THE LEGEND OF ZYE

THE LEGEND OF ZYE: X48

RACHEL CARTER

iUniverse, Inc.
Bloomington

THE LEGEND OF ZYE: X48

iUniverse books may be ordered through booksellers or by contacting:

iUniverse
1663 Liberty Drive
Bloomington, IN 47403
www.iuniverse.com
1-800-Authors (1-800-288-4677)

ISBN: 978-1-4759-3402-1 (sc)
ISBN: 978-1-4759-3404-5 (hc)
ISBN: 978-1-4759-3403-8 (e)

Library of Congress Control Number: 2012923558

Printed in the United States of America

iUniverse rev. date: 1/14/2013

TO MY FAMILY AND FRIENDS

PROLOGUE

Which thought is worse—having other planets somewhere that do support life, or being totally and completely alone in the entirety of outer space? Earth can't be alone; there has to be someone out there. But, honestly, I have no idea which I fear more. I don't mind being alone … I guess if I had to choose …

The white pen stopped scribbling over the thin lines of paper as its owner leaned back to think. The sixteen-year-old orphan Raymond Green breathed heavily and pushed his thick jet-black bangs from his heavy eyes. Bored of writing in a notebook that no one was ever going to read, he snapped it shut and reached for a book to his left. When he found his marked page, he noticed how much he'd drawn and written around the printed words. His left hand suddenly flinched, causing him to drop the book and lose his place. He growled and left the book there; he was so anxious and restless that he could barely sit down for more than a minute. Still, he couldn't leave the cramped, humid storage room, or else he wouldn't be the only one in a lot of trouble.

Raymond contented himself with watching the black sky and tiny stars through the window to his right. As silently as possible, he crawled below it and counted the stars and meteors that passed. He smiled crookedly and chuckled inwardly as he reminded himself that he was millions of miles from Earth and, for the moment, didn't have to worry about anything. He didn't have to worry about the fact that he had snuck onto the cargo area of an airplane to get from Britain to America or that he was living in an abandoned home without paying any rent because he'd scared the old family out. He didn't have to worry about breaking the law and probably going to jail for sneaking onto a NASA space shuttle. If he were found, he could be in a lot of trouble … except that no one would even know who Raymond Green was. The boy had no family, no driver's license or any other form of ID, and no papers or birth certificate—and he only spoke to one person in the entire world.

Suddenly, there was the sound of rapid footfalls from outside the door. Every drop of blood in Raymond's veins froze at once; the hallway he was in was a dead end. The only reason people came down it was to get something out of the storage room he was in. Slowly, he pressed his hands to the cool, metal flooring and twisted his body around to face the door. He held his breath and waited.

"What do you mean, I can't go in there?" said an irritable man's voice. He sounded probably thirty years of age. "It's a storage closet, Erica."

Erica, Raymond thought desperately, *I have too much luck for one kid; I pray it doesn't end now.* Erica Reins was the one person Raymond ever spoke to, and she had helped Raymond sneak onto her father's space shuttle.

"Tell me what you need," came Erica's voice, soothing and calm. "My dad told me I have to get you guys anything you want."

"You should be grateful your father allowed you to come," the man said. "It normally takes years of training to even think about going to the moon. Get me some flashlights and take them back to the cabin. Can you handle that?"

"Yes, sir." Raymond could hear both the relief and sarcasm in her voice.

There was another moment of silence as the man's heavy footfalls began and then faded into nothing. The door handle turned, and Erica stepped in, her sweeping, coppery hair flowing over one shoulder.

"Man, am I happy to see you," Raymond said, grinning. He grabbed his book and searched for his page.

"What," she said, smiling softly and sitting down beside her friend, "this book isn't enough company for you?"

"I can't just sit here for weeks," Raymond said, still flipping through the book. "I'm about to go insane!"

"I can tell that just by looking at the poor book." She took the novel from his hands and flipped through the scribbled-on pages. Coming across a strange symbol several times, she raised an eyebrow. "What is this?"

"It's a symbol of my name." He traced a finger over the lines. "It spells Raymond, see? R-A-Y-M-O-N-D."

Erica watched him point out each letter in the strange shape. It was a wide X with a vertical line through the middle. On the top right and bottom left of the X, two lines connected back to the vertical one. Raymond drew the symbol in a quick motion over the page number at the bottom, forty-eight.

"It's crazy that someone can put ten chapters into not even fifty pages," Erica noted, seeing the beginning of the tenth chapter starting at the top of the page.

"When you've got something to say, does it matter how you arrange it?" Raymond asked, pressing down the edge of the paper to mark where he was. "Chapter ten, page forty-eight … let's see if I can remember that."

Erica leaned up to kiss him on the cheek and smiled again. "I don't think you'll have a problem remembering two little numbers."

"Ten forty-eight, ten forty-eight …" he chanted under his breath. "So what do you want to do?"

"There's something I want to show you, actually," the girl said, standing up suddenly and offering Raymond a hand.

"Trust me," Raymond scoffed, taking her hand anyway, "there isn't an inch of this bloody closet you know better than me."

"But you have no idea what's outside."

"Outside what?" He raised an eyebrow.

"Outside what do you think?" She laughed.

Then it hit him. "No," he breathed, half excited, half terrified. "You're not saying I can really leave the shuttle?"

She laughed happily. "Yeah, come on … if nobody catches us." She took his hand in hers and led him down the narrow hallway into a much larger storage room. Inside, lining all four walls and the edge of the floor, were several dozen space suits, helmets, air tanks, and everything else needed in the open vacuum of space.

Raymond turned to raise an incredulous eyebrow at his friend. "What," he asked, giving her a crooked grin, "no jet packs?"

"You're hilarious," she shot sarcastically and threw him the smallest suit on the shelf.

Raymond, thin and gangly with little muscle or anything else save for bone, slid the thick, icy fabric over his white T-shirt and jeans. For a moment, he paced back and forth, just trying to get used to wearing the suit, breathing from the air tank, and speaking through a microphone that sent his voice only to Erica.

"You're not coming?" Raymond asked, realizing she hadn't changed into a suit as well. Of course she wasn't coming; she couldn't.

Raymond could see the longing in her eyes and hear the pain in her voice as she apologized. "I'm sorry. My dad told me not to leave the shuttle; I don't even know how I'm able to get away from him to see you."

Raymond nodded; he could understand that. Even though he had never met Mr. Reins face-to-face, he knew how strict of a man he was.

"Here," Erica said suddenly. Raymond hadn't even noticed she had led him to a small sliding door in the wall; the storage room they had just left was a half a hallway away. She pressed her pointer finger to a small, round button on the wall. The heavy glass doors slid smoothly into the wall, revealing a tiny white room with another door. He knew where it led.

"Thank you, Erica," Raymond said slowly. "I … I'll see you in a minute."

She smiled and then was struck with an idea. "X48," she said.

Raymond pulled the helmet from his head and shot her an inquisitive look. "What are you talking about?"

"That story you're writing in your notebook," she said. "You should call it *X48*."

"Why?" He was still confused. "It's not a story; it's just random thoughts in my head. Besides, why does it even need a title?"

"Just because you don't plan on sharing it with anyone doesn't mean it doesn't need a name," she said. "And who knows, maybe you will someday."

"All right, you've convinced me." He chuckled. "I'll call it *X48* on the tiny, unlikely chance that anyone ever knows who Raymond Green is."

She leaned up on her toes at that moment to kiss him on the lips. "I know who he is," she said when they broke apart. "He's my best friend."

"Thanks, Erica." He replaced the helmet on his head. "It's good to know one person would miss me."

"Raymond …" she said, watching him step into the little white room that would allow him to exit the shuttle. When he waited for her to continue, she shook her head and lost her train of thought. "Nothing."

The door behind Raymond slid shut, and the one before him unlocked. Slowly, almost fearfully, he slid it back and stepped outside.

There were no astronauts walking around, no labs or stations set up for research; the place was barren. There was no one there to see him. Under his thick boots, he could feel that the sand was soft and smooth. The velvety black sky was dotted with a million white stars and comets. He walked forward slowly, looking at everything all at once. *This place is beautiful,* he thought, *nothing like Earth.* Earth was loud and obnoxious, whereas this was quiet and peaceful. Raymond felt as if he could stay here for years and not tire of staring out into the nothingness of space.

He did not have years, though; he had only a few minutes before he needed to return to the shuttle. Raymond knew why he was here. Erica had helped him onto her own father's space shuttle and had hidden him there without anyone else knowing or even suspecting her actions. He was as grateful as anyone could ever be. Once again, he was hit with the realization of how little he deserved a friend like her.

Suddenly, something, like a fly bothering a horse, made him flinch violently. His thick jet-black hair fell in his face and plastered itself to his sweaty forehead. He shook his head hard, trying to remove the strands of hair from his vision, but instead did something much worse. Raymond felt more than heard a wire in the huge air tank snap apart. His breath instantly fogged up the glass, blinding him. He sucked in, trying to find air and trying not to panic, but nothing came. There was no air in his tank, and he was too far from the shuttle to run back. He felt as if he were a thousand feet under water and had lost his breath a long time ago. There was unseen pressure crushing him on all sides, and his lungs burned and seared with the lack of air; he knew he had no choice.

Unable to breathe, he reached up to the helmet, fogged up and uncomfortably hot, and pulled it off. There was a sudden, violent rush of cool air. He sucked it in desperately, not even caring that what he was doing shouldn't be possible. This, however, lasted not even a fraction of a second. In the next instant, Raymond was jerked around at a painful speed, and the helmet was wrenched from his tight grip. He could see a panic-stricken Erica staring at him, frozen in horror. Even with complete and utter terror plastered to her face, she was still beautiful. Raymond took one last glance at his best friend, the only one who would even realize he was gone. And with that, he was gone, vanished into thin air.

With the feeling of plunging through water, Raymond sped through space and time. He was jerked around and upside down. Whenever he tried to suck in a breath, his lungs felt as if they were filling with tar. Just as his lungs were about to burst, he felt himself reappear out of nothing.

Slammed hard into what felt like solid steel, he coughed hard and spat out a great deal of sand. Still unsteady, he pushed himself up, his feet scrabbling over loosely packed sand as he did so. Realizing he had landed on and broken his left wrist, he ground his teeth and clenched his fist against the fire he felt in the fractured bone.

Raymond had long since taught himself not to bend to pain, and a broken wrist wasn't anything he couldn't manage. He took a slow, deep breath and fixed his mind away from the fracture. Once the pain was gone, he realized that while the suit Erica had given him was in burned tatters, his clothes remained relatively undamaged. He shrugged ungracefully out of the remainder of the suit and pulled on the jacket that he had tied around his waist before leaving the shuttle. When he pushed the fabric over the pocket of his jeans, something small and burned fell out. He bent over and picked it up with his right hand, feeling an angry pang in his chest. It was his notebook. Allowing it to fall open, he saw that all the words were covered in black soot or burned away completely. The fragile little book was destroyed. Raymond had had the notebook since before he'd come to America; it was one thing he'd kept with him his entire life. He growled under his breath and clutched the book in his hand, accidentally crumpling it into pieces like a dead leaf in autumn. A soft breeze took it away along with the red sand at his feet.

He breathed shortly and looked around, realizing for the first time that he was not only no longer on the moon but also completely alone. He was standing on what looked and felt to be an extremely old dwarf star. It was dull red and glowing faintly but was nothing compared to what a star should be. It seemed to be made of an ocean of liquid magma with small islands scattered around. The islands were solid steel covered in a thin layer of slick red sand.

"Hello?" he shouted, not entirely knowing to whom or what he was yelling. "Is anybody out there?"

Nothing. Of course there was nothing. The only sound was the splashing of the lava against the rocks and the breeze floating around the dwarf star. Suddenly, he became aware of two things. One, if he squinted and concentrated hard, he could just make out the thin outline of something huge and round off in the distance. Two, there was a thin chain around his neck. He pulled it off and found a small pendant, almost like a dog tag but shaped differently. On one side, his name, RAYMOND GREEN, was engraved neatly into the metal. The other said KING.

A strange, crooked grin covered his lips when he read the word. *King of what, though?* he thought. He turned the pendant back over and got an answer. The tiny letters spelling out his name were gone and had been replaced with two new words: TERRA FORENSIS. Raymond knew from studying Latin that it meant land of legacy; exactly what that meant, however, he had no idea. A tiny spark of frustration touched the mass of confusion welling in his mind; nothing was making sense.

"Land of legacy," Raymond murmured under his breath. "Terra forensis, what does that …"

However, before he could even finished muttering to himself, there was a great flash of bluish-white light off in the distance where he'd seen the outline of something. The sudden burst in the almost complete darkness forced Raymond to throw one hand up to shield his eyes and stumble backward. He tripped and fell flat on his back, the dog tag flying from his grip. Something in the back of his mind told Raymond that the little tag was important, that he needed it. With instincts that he hadn't realized he possessed, Raymond caught it with his foot. He took the tag back in his hand, gripping it more tightly this time, and got gingerly to his feet; he had managed to fall once again on his broken wrist. When he was standing again, he tore off a strip of his shirt to wrap around his hand as well as possible. He looked around for the light, but it was gone. There was something new in its place.

A huge jet-black planet, maybe double or triple the size of the sun that Raymond stood on, hung lazily in the sky as if it had been there the whole time. *This dog tag must have done it,* Raymond thought, dazed. *This must be magic! That must be what I thought I saw earlier. I must have lit it up or something.*

Raymond stared back down at the tag to a new message etched into the metal. However, this time, he didn't waste time wondering; he knew what it meant. "Riding star," he said, his voice unquestioning. "Lacus sidus."

At once, a pure-white, shining star appeared gracefully barely a foot from Raymond's face. He recoiled, afraid it would burn him, but quickly realized it wasn't hot. It wasn't even warm. It was thin, flat, and very solid but cool to the touch. *Riding star,* Raymond thought, and decided not to go through a very stupid conversation with himself. With one fluid motion, he grabbed the edge of the star and pulled himself onto it in a standing position. He leaned forward, trying to find a way to balance on it, and the star shot out from under him. He landed hard and ducked when the star whipped around to meet him. Shaking slightly, he pushed himself up again and climbed back on. More carefully, he clamped on to the front of the star and leaned out again. It shot forward, but this time he stayed on, moving hundreds of thousands of miles per hour. He kept his eyes locked on the planet he'd lit up. If a planet had a sun, then it might have life—in other words, people. The wind whipping around him blew back his hair and cooled his sweaty face.

He threw his head back and laughed aloud. "*This is amazing*!" he shouted to no one and nothing, never wanting to stop, never wanting to go back to Earth.

He wasn't far from the planet when it occurred to him that this planet would need to be named. He thought for a moment and decided: the sun would be called Red, and the planet, the planet ... Several names, many in Latin, ran through his mind. He thought for a moment and remembered his last conversation with Erica. "All right, all right, you've convinced me," he had told her. "I'll call it X48 on the tiny, unlikely chance that anyone ever knows who Raymond Green is." Raymond decided. The black planet would be called X48.

1 CHAPTER ONE

"It wasn't long before Raymond Green realized the planet he had found was not empty and abandoned, as he had first thought. As he traveled over the sandy black land, he discovered animals similar to those on Earth. He saw huge eagles, wolves, and game. His riding star was too fast and too powerful to ride near the ground, and he couldn't see much from far up. After a few days, he found a tall pitch-black stallion that could move faster than any horse on Earth. He rode all night, bareback, not stopping once. By the time the sun was done rising, they had covered almost a thousand miles. At about midday, Raymond found a small tribe of humans who all spoke English and Latin. Their leader explained to Raymond that English and Latin were two of the many languages of the human species, no matter which planet they lived on. The tribe was old, unstable, and, in Raymond's eyes, well in his ability to control. He killed the old ruler and named himself king of Sandstiss. There were four tribes in total back then, as there still are. But Raymond, even with his magic and strength and power, couldn't defeat the other kings. After his first failed and humiliating attempts to conquer them, he swore he would someday rule the whole planet as his own. After almost a thousand years, everyone thought he had finally given up, but I know he never will. Now, the only things stopping Raymond from conquering the cities are the three chosen soldiers. These soldiers are handpicked from thousands by the king of their city."

"That's you, Tie," I said, interrupting my brother yet again.

Shintie allowed a small smile to curve his lips. It wasn't totally pride, but it wasn't humility, either. "I'm only a soldier, Zye," he told me. "All the other titles don't matter to me, and they shouldn't to you either."

I nodded. He always told me that pride was foolish and dangerous, but as an eight-year-old I cared only about pride and danger. As Shintie was about to leave, a man a few years younger than him suddenly blocked the doorway. I looked around my oldest brother to see my second-oldest brother, Carõ. He had the same stupid, crooked grin on his face that he always wore, his fist was curled around his sword hilt, and his dark red hair hid his eyes. He was our city's high and mighty general, kind of like Shintie. There was something so intimidating about Carõ that I shrank into Shintie's side.

"Bedtime stories for the soldier child?" Carõ asked, not hiding his sarcasm.

"Shut it, Carõ," Shintie said. "I'm trying to get him to fall asleep, not the opposite."

The general scoffed. "You don't see Ryemen needing to be talked to sleep."

Rye, my twin, was dead asleep in the other cot in the room. He was snoring and flat on his face. When the three of us glanced over, he tensed slightly as if he knew he was being watched.

"Zyemen," Carõ barked at me—he was one of the only people who used my full name regularly—"where's Father's sword?"

I lay flat on my stomach to fit my head and one arm under the cot mattress. My eyes fell on a black and scarlet sheath with a silver, diamond-encrusted hilt protruding from the end. I hooked my small fingers halfway around it and pulled it out. It was heavy and difficult to manage, and I struggled in holding it up for my brother. He took it quickly and drew it in a flourish.

"That's Zye's sword, Carõ," Shintie said with a touch of steel in his voice. He rarely got mad at anyone, but when he did it was usually at Carõ. "Father entrusted it to him."

"Of course." Carõ gritted his teeth in mock respect to his only older brother and turned to me. He slid the sword back into the sheath with such force that I was pushed backward onto my heels. Shintie glared at him.

Carõ grinned. "I just like the feel of it," he said, but even I, as an eight-year-old, could tell he was lying. "I don't understand why, out of five sons, our father would give such a powerful weapon to his youngest."

I heard a soft snarl grow in the back of Shintie's throat but ignored it; I didn't fear my oldest brother. I ducked down to replace the sword under my cot. "Good night, Carõ," I said, crawling under the thin sheet. "Good night, Shintie."

They both said good night back, Shintie slightly more kindly than Carõ, and left. Before closing the door, Shintie turned back and snapped his fingers. At once, the three candles mounted around the room went out. I heard the door click shut, and I was left in darkness. Outside my room, Shintie and Carõ continued their argument, but I was too tired to pay much attention.

2 CHAPTER TWO

Eight years later

I woke up to a hard, leather boot slamming into my face and the sound of familiar laughter not far away. I caught the shoe as it fell and chucked it back in the direction from which it had come. A second later, I heard the satisfying clunk of it connecting with its owner.

"I was sleeping, Rye," I told my twin. I turned over onto my stomach so he couldn't see my hand reach under my cot. My fingers closed round the cool metal of my sword sheath.

"And now you're awake," he said, laughing, "and you hit me in the head with my boot."

"You do the exact same thing to wake me up every day, and I'm not as strong as you," I pointed out, my voice muffled against a pillow. "You do your best to break my nose every morning."

"Wake up before me," he said, snickering, "and you won't need me to wake you up."

I grunted and jumped up from my cot in half a second. In the same amount of time, I was a foot from Rye, who was still sitting up in his bed, with my sword resting on his throat. He was ready, however. He twisted his hand under his pillow to pull out his own blade. It was shorter and heavier than mine, and I was able to back up five feet before he had a good grip on it. Rye relied more on strength than skill in sword fighting, mainly because he was self-taught, so it was more difficult than fighting a real soldier like Shintie or Carõ. We spun around the room for several minutes, blades slamming against each other over and over. Finally, I managed to hook my sword under Rye's and threw my arm up powerfully. He yelled as the end of my blade sliced his palm and his sword went flying. Baring his teeth in pain, he clamped his left hand over his bloody right and muttered something in Latin under his breath. When he let go of his hand, I saw that the gash was healed completely. He wiped his hand on his pants and went to retrieve his sword.

"How many times have you lost your sword in that way?" I asked, pulling on a shirt, boots, and belt for my sheath.

"As many times as I've healed that same exact spot," he said dryly, hiding his sword and sheath back under his pillow.

"It's amazing you don't have any scars from fighting," I noted, lacing my boots.

"It's because I'm a good healer—and a good thing too." Rye snapped his fingers to light the wall candles. "Do you know how much trouble I would be in if anyone knew I even owned a sword, let alone could hold my own against soldiers and a soldier in training?"

"Honestly, I believe everyone on X48 should own swords and know how to fight with them," I said. "I don't understand why soldiers are the only ones permitted to carry them."

"No one thinks anything is going to happen to a healer," Rye said. "And anyway, most people can use magic well enough to defend themselves without a physical weapon. I just like knowing I'm able to handle a blade."

"Who or what do you think you're going to defend yourself from?" I asked. I followed Rye toward the stairs and watched him leap headfirst over the twenty steps and land perfectly on both feet. I followed, more humanlike, after the floorboards were done rattling. I doubted that Rye was able to do the same.

"Thieves," he offered as we entered the kitchen area. "You know, those people who don't obey their tags and just don't work. Carõ says they'll slit your throat just for the change in your pocket."

"Carõ's head is full of hot air," I said, "and it's getting worse with the promotions." In the past three years, my second-oldest brother had risen from a general's adviser to a second-in-command to a fully fledged war general. I was more than confident that he hadn't entered a real battle in his life; his job was to tell the soldiers what do to. And somehow, he was very talented at that. His name was quickly becoming well known over all of Hishe and hated in Sandstiss. "It's not a choice to not follow your tag," I continued. "You can't just not attend school and training."

"Actually, you can," said a voice from behind. I turned to see Tahll, my third-oldest brother. He was actually only three years older than Rye and I. "Being born with the tags is one thing, but nothing really forces you to do what they say."

"So I don't have to be a soldier?" I asked, glancing down at the dog tag hanging from the chain on my neck. The tags that everyone on X48 owned all said two things: our names and the jobs we would grow up to do.

"You've already trained to be a soldier, Zye," said Tahll, who was a historian and teacher and had almost no sense of humor. "You can't back out now."

I watched him take a piece of thick, dark tan bread from a pan in the fireplace and lean against the table to eat it. Rye and I each took a piece. My twin managed to finish his before I had taken two bites.

"I wish I weren't a soldier," I muttered, making sure I didn't hear Shintie or Carõ coming down the stairs. "I've always wanted to be a healer."

"I know," Tahll said, shouldering a heavy-looking leather bag. "You've always said that, but you can't change what you were always meant to be."

"What's in your bag?" Rye asked, taking another piece of bread from the black and silver fire. "History essays?"

"Why would I have essays? I'm not in school," Tahll said flatly, tying a string through a hole in either side of the open bag to keep it shut. "They're letters for all the last years. Did you two honestly forget this was your final day of in-class schooling?"

"Are you joking?" Rye made a halfhearted dive for Tahll's bag. "I've been counting the days down for ten years. Give me mine!"

"You still have one final lesson today." Tahll twisted gracefully away from Rye and rested against the far wall with his black bag in between the wood and his back.

"*Tahll!*" my twin said incredulously. "No one cares about the dragon wars! Dragons are extinct. Why do you need to tell us over and over?"

"I care about the dragon wars," said Tahll coldly. He stalked toward the door, adding on the way out, "There's someone at the window."

I turned expectantly to see that he was right. It was still mostly dark outside, but from the light of the slowing rising red sun I could see the shadow of a person behind the curtain. I closed my hand to a fist, and the sheet rolled up. Through the hole in the wall I saw a sweet face waiting for us. I waved, and the girl waved back and disappeared from sight.

"O' Maari's here," I said, shouldering a bag that was much smaller than Tahll's.

"I wasn't really expecting someone else," Rye grumbled, grabbing his own bag and following me to the door. "She's the only one who comes to our house this early."

I ignored him and trotted through the doorway to meet the girl. She was two years younger than Rye and I but still in the same school year. Most of the time, no one moved up or down in the ten required years of class schooling, but somehow, O' Maari had managed to do it twice. She was sitting sidesaddle on a tall pure-white stallion named Daren. She smiled upon seeing me, pushing thick brown hair from in front of her sky-blue eyes to behind one ear. Despite being only fourteen years old, she looked and acted at least my age. She was one of the youngest in Hishe to finish school in over five hundred years.

"Good morning, O' Maari," I said, stroking Daren's slick neck.

"Good morning, Zye," she said and smiled, almost laughing. "Good morning, Rye. Is Tahll okay? He left your barn on his horse pretty fast."

"I was trying to explain to him how useless history is," Rye said. O' Maari slipped off her horse's back and he walked behind the three of us to my family's barn.

"Tahll's a historian," O' Maari said obviously. "I would think he enjoys history."

"Leave the past in the past," Rye said grumpily, pushing open the barn doors.

My family's stable comprised one long hallway of stalls and side rooms. There were ten occupied and three empty stalls. One was for my mother's horse, five for mine and my brothers', and another for our groom's, Razor. The other three were war horses: my father's, Carõ's, and Shintie's. The side rooms were for tack, feed, and other equipment that, most of the time, only Razor worried about. Inside, I saw him in his own horse's stall, filling her water trough.

"Razor," I said as soon as he was in earshot.

He looked up and pushed his sweaty brown hair from his face. "Sir?"

"Are Star and Mason tacked?"

"Yes, sir," he said, stepping out of the stall and hanging a metal bucket on a hook. "Starra is in her stall, and Mason is in a tie down the hall."

"Thanks, Raz," Rye said happily, trotting down toward a cross tie. Standing in it was a tall, Arabian dun kicking angrily at nothing in particular.

I stepped over to a wide stall door and pulled it back. Inside was a jet-black thoroughbred with a perfect, nine-point star on her forelock. I took the reins in one hand and led the mare into the hall, where I had enough room to climb on.

"Why don't you just tack up your horses yourself?" O' Maari muttered in an undertone. "It takes ten minutes to brush a horse and throw a saddle on."

"My father was wealthy enough to hire a groom," I said, shrugging. "This way I can sleep for five more minutes."

"You mean fence with Rye?" She raised an eyebrow.

"What is that supposed to mean?" I asked defensively.

"Nothing at all." Her voice was cold and bitter. Sword fighting was always a bad topic to talk about with her. "It's just, if a healer can learn to fight, I don't understand why a girl can't."

"Because no one knows he can fight," I said.

I put one foot in a saddle iron and pulled myself up. O' Maari, still disgruntled, took a handful of Daren's mane and leapt easily onto his white back. Rye, already mounted, was spinning Mason in quick, tight circles, trying to calm him.

"Didn't you ever train him yourself when you were little?" asked O' Maari.

"No one can train this horse," Rye grunted, losing an iron and almost slipping sideways to the ground. "Even Zye and Shintie couldn't."

O' Maari laughed and sifted her hand through her horse's mane. "Come on," she said happily, "I'll race you two."

"You're on." I pressed my heels sharply to the thoroughbred's muscular sides and felt her smooth leap into an immediate full gallop. Her velvet mane whipped my face as I lay flat against her spine, willing her faster. I didn't even look back to see where Daren and Mason were; I knew they had no chance of passing me. Starra was as good as a war horse. Daren was a traveling horse, and Mason was just uncontrollable. We were both trained to be able to travel more than seventy miles each hour without stopping. The thirty-mile trip to my school was done easily in under half an hour.

When Starra and I, as always, were the first to arrive at the school, I climbed off and tied her reins to a post. The sun was still low in the sky, and the school was, so far, totally empty. Even though Tahll had left before us, he was almost always the last to arrive. His old stallion only walked, and even if he could have cantered, Tahll couldn't make him. I leaned lightly against Starra's side and waited for my brother and best friend, glaring through the dark window into the school room.

The school was composed of only one square room with several tables that were arranged in neat rows. The teachers stood for the entire lesson, lecturing about whichever topic they felt like teaching that day. For five to six hours, one teacher would talk and students would take notes. No speaking or standing was ever allowed.

I was unsure of just how many schools there were in Hishe, but I did know that all of them were run exactly the same as the others. Students aged fifteen and sixteen were taught for six hours starting at sunrise. Students aged ten to fourteen were taught for six hours directly after us, when the sun was right overhead. Students aged five to nine were taught from when the second class ended until nightfall, about four hours later.

With Rye and O' Maari still a few minutes behind me, I sauntered into the classroom. It was almost completely dark inside, and I had to snap my fingers to light some of the wall candles to find my table. I weaved through to it and dropped my bag onto the surface. At that moment, I heard soft hooves approaching at a light canter. I stepped back outside to meet O' Maari and Daren.

"How long have you been here?" she said, still sidesaddle as before.

"A few hours," I said, laughing. "No different than any other day."

"Oh, shut it." She glared for a second and then laughed and returned my smile. She leapt from Daren's shoulder on the right side and tied him next to Starra. The two horses nickered back and forth as if talking, and Daren nipped playfully as Starra's mane. They had known each other as long as O' Maari and I had known each other, more than nine years.

"Where's Rye?" I jerked my head to the side to remove the dark red hair hanging in my face. "Still at the barn? Or did Mason bolt again?"

"He's on his way," O' Maari said, fingering Daren's mane. "Mason isn't a racehorse."

"Neither is Starra," I said, patting her on the neck. "She just knows how to run."

"Mason knows how to run all right," she said, slightly serious. "He just doesn't know how to run with a person on his back."

"Or Rye doesn't know how to stay on."

"That's not fair," she snapped. "You and Shintie can't ride him either."

I shrugged and leaned against Starra while we waited for Rye and the remainder of the class. The sun had fully risen, and three-quarters of the students had arrived before O' Maari spotted a dull, limping figure coming down the street. Rye was angrily jerking on Mason's reins, dodging the horse's massive head when he reared up. There was a wide rip in the shoulder of Rye's shirt, and he was covered head to foot in dust. There was a shallow cut bleeding slowly on his forehead, and his hair was plastered to his head with water. Before he was in earshot, the stallion had reared up four times. He walked right past us without saying a word and tied his horse tightly to the post.

"I hate horses," Rye said when he returned. "That stupid mule of a stallion dragged me for half a mile. Some soldier finally got him to stop, but he has way too much energy. Zye, can you help me out here?" He gestured to his dusty clothes.

I smirked, twisted my wrist around, and pointed it straight out toward my brother. A blast of cold air hit Rye, and the dirt blew off. His hair spiked out backward as it dried. The spell worked fairly well, but the cut was still bleeding steadily. He healed it by muttering some Latin that I didn't understand and wiped away most of the blood with his sleeve. We walked into the school just as Tahll was riding up.

"Did you get lost, Brother?" Rye asked, grinning at the man.

Tahll glared at him. "You are one to talk about getting lost on horseback."

"I didn't get lost, though," my twin said. "I fell off. There's a difference."

"Is it possible that if you didn't try and keep up with a war horse, you might not fall off every time you got on?" Tahll asked, taking papers from his bag and organizing them on the front desk.

"I don't try," Rye defended himself weakly. "As soon as he sees someone take off, Mason wants to follow."

Tahll pressed his lips together in lack of amusement. "Can you find your desk, please?" he asked, adding almost sarcastically, "*Brother*."

After a moment, Rye snorted and went back up to his seat.

"Now that we can begin," Tahll said dryly, clasping his hands behind his back, "could everyone take a seat. You two, the table isn't a footrest." The teacher's voice was quick and sharp, the kind of voice that got quite annoying after a few minutes—and we had to listen to him for six hours a day. Rye and a dark-haired boy behind us (the two Tahll had been referring to) sat up and retrieved pens and notebooks from their bags.

"Right then, now that everyone is settled, I would like to first congratulate the students who are finishing school for good today." He paused to see if he would get a response but only created an awkward silence. "Remember, however, you all have one more day. Does everyone have their notes out? Good, all right. I believe we left off last week with the battle of the dragon masters. As you should know, dragons are now completely extinct, but when they did live on X48, most had masters or riders."

I glanced over at O' Maari, who was writing Tahll's words exactly with amazing speed. Without ever looking down, she kept perfectly straight lines in a neat, slanted cursive. I watched her, mesmerized, for several minutes before I realized I hadn't heard a word of my brother's speech. I shook my head to clear my thoughts and forced my face down and my hand to a blank page.

A little more than six hours later, Tahll ended his lecture and dismissed the younger students. I signed heavily and arched my stiff right hand, sliding my things back into my bag with my left. Around me, everyone else was doing much of the same, apart from Rye. My twin was asleep, snoring softly with his head upside down against the back of the chair. He had about three-quarters of one page of notes written; I had finished the front and back of seven. I glanced over at O' Maari, who had a stack of papers probably ten or eleven high and was still writing. As I waited for her, I watched my brother's steady breathing, wondering how deeply asleep he was. He wasn't snoring very loudly, so he couldn't be too gone. However, after ten years of practice, he had mastered sleeping in school. I hooked my foot under his leaning chair and tilted it backward. Rye's eyes snapped open, and he yelled out as he fell fast. His head connected with the table behind him. He sat still on the floor for a moment, dazed and confused, and rubbed the back of his head painfully.

About a half of a second later, he launched at me, wrapping his arms around my legs and knocking me over. We stayed down for a short moment, wrestling playfully. I was smaller than Rye but faster, so it was easy to dodge around him and pin his arms. On the other hand, my brother was stronger and knew how to manipulate his strength. The first time I had one of his thick arms behind his back, it was almost too easy for him to simply move it back in front of him as if I weren't even there.

"Will you two knock it off?" said a voice suddenly.

We froze, Rye with his arm around my neck, and looked up to see Tahll standing over us. He was frowning impatiently and holding our letters in one hand.

"Ah, I forgot about those." Rye smoothed out his ruffled hair and snatched his letter from Tahll. "Thanks, Brother."

"Here, Zye." Tahll handed me the folded paper, and I opened it slowly. Inside were only a few words:

Name: Zyemen
Occupation: Soldier
Training Ground: Silver Canyon
Arrive at the main gate of the Walls of Hishe at sunset in two days. Bring minimum clothing and a horse (required). No exceptions.

I sighed heavily; the main gate was almost a twelve-hour trip from where I lived in the city. I would have to leave tomorrow morning to make it there on time and not be exhausted. Silver was a huge canyon used to train soldiers, and it was also the deepest canyon on X48. I'd never seen it in real life, but it was said that you couldn't see the bottom when standing at the top. I tried to imagine such a thing and failed.

"Zye!"

I snapped out of my reverie and back to the classroom. O' Maari, Rye, and I were the only ones left in the vicinity; even Tahll was gone, and O' Maari was staring at me with some concern, "What?" I asked, folding the parchment into a tiny square and sliding it into my bag. I glanced over at Rye; he was, amazingly, asleep again.

"Zye," it had been O' Maari who said my name, "are you all right?"

"Yeah," I muttered, standing and running a hand through my hair, "just fine."

"I swear, you and Rye doze off faster than anyone I know," she said, shaking my brother's shoulder to wake him up.

"I wasn't asleep. I was thinking," I said, leading the way outside.

"About what?"

"About how big and far off Silver is."

"When do you have to leave?"

"Either tonight or tomorrow morning." I pulled myself easily into Starra's saddle. "I have to be at the main gate in two days."

"Nice trip," she mused.

"Might as well get used to a trip like that now rather than on your way to a real battle."

"Why don't you leave in the morning so we can have one last campfire tonight?" O' Maari asked, climbing onto Daren and untying his and Starra's reins.

"I think I'm going to take you up on that." I smiled, turning Starra in a quick circle. "Will I meet you at the forest edge at sundown?"

She nodded and offered her hand, which I kissed softly. With my reins in both hands, I spurred my mare's sides and clucked my tongue. She took off at once on the correct road. I cued her to speed up and bent low over her neck, preparing. Her reaction was quicker than lightning, sudden and smooth. The mare could feel my weight even out and picked up her speed; transitioning from an even canter to a full-out gallop. Actually, full-out gallop is an understatement—by a lot. Starra was named not only for her markings but also for her speed; she could almost keep pace with a riding star, something no other horse, even a wild one, could do. I was on my way, if I hadn't previously mentioned, to physical training for being a soldier. Today was my final day not only in a classroom but also with my trainer. The trip from the school was over sixty miles away, and Starra and I covered the ground in less than fifty minutes.

"Sorry," I said as soon as my trainer was in earshot. He was standing calmly at the edge of the training grounds. His short blond hair spiked in every direction, and his thickly muscled arms made him look about ten years younger than he really was. Tayer watched me leap from Starra's saddle and run over to him. I trusted my horse not to bolt off and didn't tie her up. "Sorry," I repeated when I was closer. I was a little more than an hour late, but Tayer trusted that I had been at school during that hour.

"Don't apologize, Zye." Tayer's voice was strong and sharp; he wasn't a soldier, but he could have been. "Shintie was late far more than you."

I grinned despite myself. I was like Shintie, not Carõ, and that didn't seem to be changing anytime soon. I respected Carõ and his skill as a leader, but I couldn't stand it when I was compared to him. Tayer understood what I felt and always referred to my oldest, favorite brother. He had, in fact, trained all three of us.

"How was your final day of school?" Tayer asked conversationally.

"Dull," I said, watching him carefully. "It always is."

"Are my lessons dull?"

"No, not at all." My hand flinched slightly as if something in the back of my mind were telling me to draw my sword. "You are an excellent instructor."

"Thank you."

That was it. Before the second word had finished on his lips, Tayer had taken out his blade and swiped it at my stomach. I shouted in slight surprise and jumped backward about five feet. I was able to regain only enough ground to draw my sword before he advanced quickly and twisted around me in a tight circle. I stood solidly, unable to gain ground but able to not lose any.

"Never expect what you expect to happen," Tayer said. "You were too tensed up waiting for me to attack, so when I did your brain freaked you out."

I gave a nod of acknowledgment and tried hard to focus. It was difficult because Tayer liked to continue a conversation during our lessons. "What is my goal now?" I asked. There was always something to accomplish with Tayer's lessons; we never just started fencing for the sport of it.

"There's a key on a silver chain on my neck," he explained. "Do you see it?"

I nodded.

"Do anything necessary to gain possession of it," he continued. "Your only rules are, you can't break the chain or use any magic."

"Yes, sir," I said, making a point not to grumble about the no-magic rule. Tayer never allowed me to use magic; he said that it was a cheater's tool for a soldier and that wars were not won with unfair advantages. We both knew the statement was untrue.

I focused on the bout. Tayer didn't rely on physical strength like Rye. His sword fighting was quite similar to mine in the sense that we both had a lighter, quicker style. Tayer and I used more skill and ability, which made defeating each other difficult. I compared the experience to what fencing myself would probably be like. According to him, I was fast but still managed to maintain the power in my grip that those who relied on strength alone used.

Several times in the first few minutes of the lesson, I made a mad grab for the chain on Tayer's neck but missed. Once, my middle finger wrapped partly around it, but that attempt earned me a sword hilt to the face, so I was forced to let go. Getting slightly frustrated, I flicked my wrist up and over, beating Tayer's blade to the left and stepping closer. He jumped back, parrying aggressively and forcing me to back up so quickly that I tripped and fell flat on my back. I tucked into a quick ball and propelled myself backward to my feet, getting angrier. For the following thirty seconds, Tayer and I fought powerfully and energetically as each of us tried to land a blow. After two full minutes, I was able to slide my foot forward and kick Tayer in the back of the heel. It wasn't enough to trip him, but it did catch him off guard. I jumped to the side to push the flat of my foot against his lower leg, and he fell fast and hard. I heard a sickening crack as he landed. I leaned forward, hooking a finger around the chain and removing it from his neck. I held it in one hand, satisfied with my prize, and held out a hand to my instructor.

"Why offer assistance to your enemy?" he asked, accepting my hand and getting to his feet.

I sheathed my sword and handed the chain back to him. "There is nothing more humiliating to a soldier than defeat," I said. "Only an ounce of sportsmanship could help."

"Sportsmanship would only worsen the blow—and besides, you're not going to be showing sportsmanship on a battlefield, are you?" Tayer asked.

But I already had an answer for that. "I'm not going to be fighting a good friend to the death," I said.

Tayer's face became dark and serious, and his hand tightened over his hilt. "Never say that, Zye," he said. "You never know when your words will betray you."

"What if that were to arise?" I asked, suddenly concerned.

Tayer's expression softened, and he relaxed his stance. "Zye, if you ever find yourself sword to sword with someone, you know there are just two questions you ask yourself. One, what am I fighting a man I know for? And two, what is a man who knows me fighting me for? Answer those and you'll choose which side wins."

"Thank you, sir," I said. "It really is an honor having you as a teacher."

Tayer, however, didn't seem to hear me. He was staring toward the end of the training ground, where there was something off in the distance. After a short moment, it was recognizable: seven men galloping on horses, heading right toward us.

"Tayer?" I asked cautiously. My voice sounded strange.

"I know these men." Tayer's voice was low and dark. "They're trouble."

I nodded slowly and watched them approach. They were riding quickly and definitely toward us; there was no one around for miles. The look on Tayer's face, anxious and almost worried, confirmed my suspicion that their arrival wasn't a good thing.

3
CHAPTER THREE

The horses came on quickly, reaching us in a matter of minutes. Up close, I was able to tell that the riders weren't guards or soldiers of any kind. They wore aged clothing and sheaths covered in dust and deep scratches. All of them rode bareback, and only two used reins, but all of them were skilled, dangerous-looking riders. They formed a thin V, with their leader stopping feet from Tayer. The two men snarled at each other.

"It's been a long time, Tayer." The man in the front of the group spoke with a gruff, sharp voice; he was thin and tall with thick jet-black hair and a short beard. As he spoke, the rest of the riders fanned out into a circle around the two of us. After a moment, he noticed me. "Is this your newest student?"

"I have no time for you now, Hiean." Tayer's voice was angry, quick, and abrupt as I'd never heard it before. "I am very busy."

The man named Hiean laughed. "Surely you can spare a minute to an old friend?"

"You are not my friend, and I have no minute." I watched Tayer's hand flinch back an inch toward his hilt. "Now, you and your brothers, off my land! Now!"

The other six men dismounted in one second, all at once, and, in the same motion, drew swords. Their horses backed away several paces, and Starra, waiting about a hundred yards off, galloped up to herd them away. When they saw her, most of them did flee the line of fire. I heard the metallic sliding of Tayer's blade against its sheath and drew mine as well. The atmosphere had changed: the air was thicker, tenser, with the prospect of an oncoming fight.

Hiean smirked, "Still so quick to the sword, aren't you, Tayer?"

"What do you want, old man?" Tayer asked, leaning back on his heels. I wasn't exactly sure how much room Tayer had to call Hiean an old man, but I wasn't about to side with the unwelcome visitor.

"I want the key you're holding," he said simply, watching Tayer replace the chain around his neck and behind his dog tag. "It's golden, isn't it?"

"It doesn't matter what it is made of," my teacher said, still calm. "You and your brothers have jobs. Why not work for gold instead of taking my teaching tools?"

"This is easier," said one of Hiean's brothers excitedly, and Tayer laughed.

"If you give me the key without a fight, your little soldier boy can die in an actual battle and not now," Hiean said coolly.

I sneered and held up my sword, welcoming the fight. Tayer closed his eyes in thought for a moment and then opened them with new aggression.

"Very well," the older man said and addressed his brothers. "Kill both of them."

"Zye," Tayer said, "I hope I've taught you enough to fight for real."

"So do I," I said as the seven swordsmen closed in.

Two of the men came at me and four at Tayer. Hiean watched from a safe distance. My two opponents were large, muscled, and fast but not skilled. They took heavy, violent swipes with thick blades and mainly relied on strength. After ducking a fast swing at my head, I twisted around, grabbed the first man's arm, and held it behind his back. Holding on to his shoulder, I jumped forward to kick his blade free. It landed almost twenty feet away. I landed in front of him and twisted my sword in my hand to hit him over the head with the hilt. He fell, dazed but conscious, and I turned back to the second man. He was taller than the first but not so muscled, and his sword was longer and thinner. Keeping my arm steady, I advanced quickly and engaged him like a fencer. He realized what I was doing and ran forward with the same speed as myself. I threw my arm forward and dodged him, but he just did the exact same thing. He then jumped forward and spun my sword powerfully—maybe not a very mature move but nonetheless effective. My hand, slippery from sweat and already tired, almost released my sword's hilt as it was spun in fast circles. I forced my way forward, and he stumbled backward clumsily. With the slight advantage, I took the second of rest to switch sword hands. I wasn't as strong with my left, but my right was too tired to continue. I ran forward again, hoping he might think I was really left-handed and change style. He did. He swung wildly to the left to push my blade over, offering a clear shot to his body. I threw up a booted foot and planted it against his chest. The power of the blow knocked him back, and he fell hard, his head slamming against the stiff, sandy ground. He lay stunned for a few seconds, the air gone from his lungs, and coughed on dust.

I whipped around to face the next man, but the other four were all circling Tayer. One was, anyway. One was lying facedown in the sand, another was down but relatively unharmed, and the third was gone. I watched Tayer and the final man for half a moment. In less than a minute, the last opponent was down and chasing after his sword, which had been launched up and away with extended force. Finally, my teacher faced Hiean, and both men smiled. They moved their arms forward slowly so that the tips of the blades touched for a second as they bowed respectfully. Then, both of them exploded at once. Their swords moved fast and violently, and they spun on the spot, each man's feet landing within millimeters of the other's but never touching. I saw Hiean's blade pass right over Tayer's shoulders and catch the silver chain of the key. It snapped and fell to the ground, splashing in the sand. As the two moved away from the spot, I dove for the key and wrapped the broken chain around my hand so as not to drop it. I then shut my eyes for a second, took a breath, and launched myself toward Hiean.

The only thing that froze me in my tracks to the sandy ground was Hiean's next move. He beat Tayer's sword away with a hard final jerk of the entire arm, a move clearly illustrating that he was relying more on strength than skill. With a low gasp of exhaustion and pain, Tayer relinquished his slack grasp on the hilt. The sword landed only two feet away, but that was enough. My instructor fell, landing on his back, and was defenseless.

Hiean knelt down beside Tayer and took hold of the shoulder of his shirt, lifting his torso off the ground. He rested his sword against the old man's neck and grinned. "I guess you are growing old, aren't you, my friend? That was so easy, it was hardly enjoyable."

Enjoyable? I thought, appalled. *What kind of man considers killing enjoyable?*

But then both men were grinning, and Hiean sheathed his sword to take Tayer's arm and pull him to his feet. Tayer retrieved his own blade and laughed at the man who had, up until a few seconds ago, had been planning on killing him.

"What's going on?" I asked, staring between the two men.

"This was your final test, Zye," Tayer said, stepping over to me, "and you have passed."

Trying to keep up, I stuttered, "He doesn't want to kill you?"

"Of course not," Hiean added. "Tayer is my greatest friend; I was merely doing him a favor by seeing your skills when you thought you and he were in real danger."

"Well, then, if you don't have the intention of killing us, I believe I must thank you for helping me in my training," I said, nodding at Hiean and his brothers.

The man turned his head toward the horses they had come on, now grazing contently in the field not far away. He placed his pointer and middle finger in his mouth and whistled shrilly, demonstrating a talent that many people had—though not me. At the sound, all seven heads shot up, and the horses cantered over.

"It was no problem, no trouble at all." Hiean mounted his horse and turned the high-strung Arab in a quick circle. "I feel more comfortable knowing there's at least one talented soldier out on the field."

I rolled my eyes slightly in order to shrug off the compliment and turned back to Tayer. "By the way, I almost forgot to ask you: my mother asked me to invite you to dinner, as it's my last night here for a long time."

"I would love to come, Zye," Tayer said, looking disappointed, "but I'm going to talk to a young man in a prison across the East End of Hishe."

Hiean let out an angry huff of exasperation. "You can't change that boy, Tayer," he said dryly. "There is something seriously wrong with him; not even you could talk sense into him."

"He's only thirteen." Tayer crossed his arms over his chest, not in a hostile way but as something to do, and said, "And I'm not just going to talk to him. I'm going to teach him how to use a sword; it might give him something to do while he's locked in a cell all day and night."

"And you're under what delusion that Zhyer would ever be allowed to touch a weapon again?"

"I'm sorry, but who's Zhyer?" I asked before Tayer could retaliate.

"A criminal," Hiean answered. He nodded to his brothers, who took off at a full gallop. "He's a poor, no-good thief and a pathetic excuse for a Hishe citizen. He's stolen from food markets and banks and weapon holds, set fire to houses, freed half an army's stable of horses. Anything else you can think of, he has probably done."

"Why? What would be the cause for anyone to do something like that?"

"His father died when he was young, and right away it changed him; he refused to go to school or eat or ride or even leave his room. By the time he was ten, he no longer lived with his family and ate what was left in market areas."

"My father died when I was very young," I pointed out. "And I didn't lose it. But still, why a weapon hold? He could be killed." In the back of my mind, I could picture the heavily guarded, solid iron-walled building. There was only one key to each one, and it was almost always kept in position of Rainwin, the king of Hishe. At all hours of the day and night, it was surrounded by over fifty mounted guards and hundreds on foot. I'd seen it only once before, when I was five and Carõ took me with him to see the inside. As a high general, Carõ had permission to request for Rainwin to unlock the hold. Upon seeing me, a five-year-old soldier-to-be, the guards were reluctant to let me in; normally, only one or two people entered at once. Rainwin told them to let me pass, and of course they obeyed, but they grumbled under their breath doing so.

Inside the hold were hundreds upon thousands of weapons, kinds I'd never even tried to imagine. Swords and bows and arrows were obvious, but along with those were spears, ice rods, clubs, whips, chains, bombs, poison, and so on. I had followed Rainwin and Carõ, talking anxiously about an upcoming battle against a kind of people called Draes, to a row of small glass vials. They were filled to the brim with a clear liquid that seemed almost thinner than water.

"One will do," Rainwin had told him. "Draes may appear strong, but when it comes down to it, they are very weak. One drop on your sword will be enough to last even an army as great as this."

I had watched Carõ take the vial and place it safely in his bag. He looked solemnly at Rainwin and said, "Not all are as weak as you might think, sir."

"I know of whom you are speaking of, Carõ, and you are correct. But he is the only one I've met strong enough and brave enough to leave." Rainwin sighed and placed a momentary hand on Carõ's shoulder. "You do know he only did it to protect you and your brothers, right?"

"I know that." Carõ brushed past the king and me and stared at the door. "It just angers me; he left without even any good-bye, without anything."

Carõ had never told me the meaning of his conversation. I still knew very little about Draes, only that they were very strong and very hard to kill. As far as I knew, though, I had never known one. I didn't think Carō had either, but there were many things he liked to keep from me.

"He doesn't have anything left to live for," came Hiean's sharp voice. It seemed almost far away. I refocused my attention to the present conversation. "I don't think he cares whether he lives or dies anymore."

"Didn't he have a job on his dog tag?" I asked.

"He melted it," said Tayer icily. "He's lucky doing that didn't kill him; your tag is who you are. It would be the same as melting off your leg or something."

"He melted it," I repeated, dumbfounded. "I didn't even think that was possible!"

"If they get hot enough," Hiean said, turning the restless Arab in another quick circle, "they will melt. They aren't indestructible, Zye."

"I've always pictured them as such." The tiny metal tag around my neck suddenly felt quite fragile and weak. I tucked it under my shirt.

Hiean glanced at Tayer. "I really must be on my way now. It was nice to see you again and to meet you, Zye."

He clicked to his horse, who was all too excited to take off. He bolted from the field as if it had been lit on fire and was out of sight in less than a minute.

"Well, Zye." Tayer and I began walking toward the edge of training field, where Starra and Tayer's horse stood grazing contently. "It was an honor training you, but you don't need me anymore. You've become quite an accomplished fighter and rider."

"Thank you, Tayer." I pulled myself up onto Starra's back, feeling that she was tense with excitement at the prospect of galloping. "I hope to see you again."

"Don't worry, Zyemen. You will."

I clicked softly to the mare, and she took off at once. Her mane flew back to whip me in the face, and behind me her tail waved out almost completely straight. I absolutely loved riding Starra; she was so fast, it felt like flying, and any gait or transition was as smooth as water. The rest of the world was only a blur at her full gallop, and there was not a horse alive that could match her speed. She was the most graceful animal on X48 (and anywhere else as well), and she knew it. At a slower pace, she would prance and throw her front legs as far forward as possible without tripping and hold her head up pressed to her neck. Rye would often call us a proper English pair because of how exactly we were able to ride if both of us were trying.

I arrived back at my family's stable after only about twenty minutes, almost half the time Rye and Mason could manage even when he didn't get thrown off. The horses whinnied loudly at the sound of Starra's hooves on the hard pavement, and the mare responded with a pleasant nicker. She trotted over to Mayan, Carō's stallion and her father, and waited for me to dismount. I did, sliding gracefully from her back, and glanced around for Razor. I saw him a moment later, returning from the pasture with Mason. He had the leading line in one hand and the halter in the other, attempting to control the wild Arab. The fifteen-year-old groom threw all the weight of his shoulder at Mason and jumped out of the way when the horse retaliated by throwing his head wildly and making his best attempt to crush Razor's feet. Razor kicked open Mason's stall door with one foot and dodged out of the way as the stallion barged his way through. With one hand, Razor pushed his copper-brown hair from his eyes and walked over. I noticed that his other hand was bleeding lightly from a rope burn.

"You're going to have to let me know," Razor said breathlessly, "if your brother ever gets a horse that walks in a straight line for two seconds—or walks at all, for that matter."

"I'll be sure to let you know, Razor." I smiled; it comforted me slightly to know that Razor couldn't control Mason either.

The young groom took Starra's reins from me. "I would greatly appreciate it," he said, giving me a half grin. "This horse is a …"

I raised one eyebrow, and he stopped himself, "Anyway," I said, turning to the barn door, "I'll be back in about an hour; you can leave Starra in if you want to."

"Oh, I'm not letting them out," Razor said quickly, "I was lunging this crazy Arab; he has to burn some energy somehow."

I nodded. "She's probably too tired anyway. Is your hand all right?"

"It's fine." He rapped it in a piece of cloth. "It's an occupational hazard."

I laughed and walked from the barn. Razor's occupational hazard was a rope burn; mine was dying. The walk from the barn to my house was less than a quarter of a mile, and I covered it in a few minutes. By the time I reached the front door, the huge sun that hung over X48 was beginning to fade into the wall of Hishe. The sun, by the way, was called Red. It wasn't yet dark out; however, it was no longer light as day.

I pushed the door open that led into the eating room to see my family sitting there waiting for me. My mother was seated at the very end of the table as the head. That position was usually taken by the father, but seeing as we didn't have one, my mother took the post. To her right sat Shintie, as the oldest, and then Carõ, Tahll, Rye, and an empty seat. That empty seat was mine. The chairs wrapped around the table so that I was seated to the very left of my mother. She nodded when she saw me enter, and I hurried over, quickly taking my place in between her and Rye.

"So, Rye, Zye," my mother said, beaming at us as we passed plates of food around, "I'm so proud of both of you. Now I have five men who have all graduated schooling on their first try. You know, my father had to repeat ninth year."

Rye laughed. "Yeah," he said happily, "you told us about that."

"We're not yet of age, though," I reminded my mother. "Two more years."

"Wow," Shintie chimed in, "how on X48 can you two be sixteen already? You guys have to go back to schooling for another couple of years; you *can't* be done."

Tahll choked on his drink. "Oh, yes, I would love teaching Rye for another two years; he was a pain in the—anyway, congratulations, you two."

The conversation continued on, the whole time Carõ not saying a word. The only thing that really ended the pleasant chat was a thought that came to my mind when I was speaking of my last day of training.

"Carõ," I said. He glanced up from his almost untouched plate. "The weapon hold came up when I was talking to Tayer today. I remembered that day I went there with you and Rainwin; I was wondering, who were you talking about?"

"I don't know what *you're* talking about," he retaliated quickly, his voice hard and on edge. "I've been in the weapon hold hundreds of times. How could I possibly …"

"You and Rainwin were talking about a Draes and took a small vial of a clear liquid from the hold," I interrupted him sharply. "Rainwin told you that you would only need one because they were ultimately weak."

As I said this, I could see the recognition dawning in his face. I could tell, even if he didn't admit it, that he knew exactly what I was talking about. As I waited for his response, the table grew silent. No one moved. Carõ wasn't glaring at me, but it was close. He was frowning with one eyebrow raised, waiting for me to say something.

"It doesn't matter who I was talking about, Zye." There was ice in his voice. "It doesn't concern you at all. Don't worry about it."

"Why am I not allowed to know?" I asked heatedly. "Is this someone I know already? Carõ, answer me."

I really didn't like getting on the wrong side of my brothers, and Carõ especially, but he was driving me too far. I was honestly trying to stay calm, but his next remark made my blood boil. The one thing I couldn't stand to hear.

"When you're older," he said, taking a calming breath. "You're too young."

"*I'M SIXTEEN!*" I shouted angrily, losing all patience. I stood up, kicking my chair back against the wall. "*How dare you!*"

"Boys!" my mother said sharply. "Zyemen, sit down, now."

"You *don't* need to know." Carõ gritted his teeth but was otherwise composed; he was quite talented at holding back his anger. "I *don't* want you to know."

"If you can know, than why can't I?" I asked, still standing but not shouting anymore. "Or Rye? Or Tahll or Shintie? Or do they already know? Am I the last one left in the dark, like I usually am?"

From the corner of my eye, I saw Tahll roll his eyes, but I was too angry to care.

"Shintie knows." Carõ nodded; he seemed content now that I wasn't as angry anymore. "Now do you want to sit back down so we can finish our meal?"

If the comment about my age hadn't turned my face red, that did. The knife I had been clutching in my hand suddenly sliced into my palm; my fingers had closed around it into a fist. I didn't feel the pain of the blade cutting my skin, just the pain of Carõ's last remark freezing the blood in my body on the spot.

Carõ had done this a lot more when we were younger, and more as a joke, but now it was different. Even to Shintie, he acted as if he were the oldest, the strongest, and the wisest. He would sit at the head of the table (that's why my mother sat there instead of the other end, because Carõ considered himself the highest) and act as our father. Now, he was doing it again, and it drove me over the edge.

"Shut up," I said. My voice was calm but full of menace. "You are so in love with your power that you forget when it goes away!"

"Fine," Carõ said shortly. "You honestly want to know who the Draes was who I was talking about?"

I nodded. I was still standing, but my shoulders had relaxed some.

Complete and total silence filled the room for almost an entire minute; Carõ and I were still glaring at each other. "Father," he spat finally. He left then, the door rattling in its hinges behind him.

4 CHAPTER FOUR

I made to follow him immediately, not even so much as glancing back at the rest of my family. My father couldn't be a Draes; he couldn't. Draes couldn't die, and my father had died thirteen years ago … or so Carō had always told me. What if my father was alive? What if he was somewhere outside the city as a Draes? I shook my head and ran after my brother. About halfway down the road, I saw him disappear into our barn and slam shut the heavy door. It rebounded back a half foot and was pulled back again with a soft click. I hurried toward it, half-afraid he would take Mayan. I really wasn't in the mood to chase anyone on Starra. I never saw him leave, though, so I could only assume he was still there, probably doing his best not to destroy anything out of anger. He'd once punched his room door so hard that it had splintered in on itself. The only good thing about him being in a barn was that the doors and walls were a lot thicker.

When I reached the door, I found it to be bolted from the inside. I pulled out my sword, slid it through the crack between the wall and the door, and forced the wooden bolt up. When I knew it was high enough, I leaned the blade to the right to wedge the heavy door open and pulled it back the rest of the way with my free left hand. Inside, the barn was dimly lit and empty-looking; Razor had obviously left for the night. The horses whinnied happily when they saw me, and Starra stuck her head out from her stall and nickered loudly to be patted. I strolled over to her, sword still in hand, and stroked her graceful head.

"You know, I used to be jealous of you inheriting that sword," came Carō's voice from nowhere.

I whipped around to see him leaning against Mayan's stall door. His arms were crossed over his chest, and his dark hair covered his upper face, but he looked for the most part calmed down.

"Now I realize it's a good thing I didn't get it," he continued. "I could have been cursed like you."

"What are you talking about?" I demanded. Why was his voice so demented?

"You don't understand," he said, standing up straight. There was an air of mock concern in his voice. "Our father was a Draes. That means one of us is too."

I froze in place and sucked in an airless breath; everything in my mind was suddenly nonexistent save for that one little fact. I stared in shock at my brother and, knowing I wouldn't like whatever answer he gave me, asked the question anyway. "Who?"

Carõ sighed long and low, and there was almost a look of sick satisfaction on his face. "Let me give you a hint," he said. "It isn't Shintie, it isn't Tahll, and it isn't your twin."

"Me." I breathed. "I'm a Draes?"

Carõ nodded, "Father said he was always better off dead; he never wanted to have the life he did. He was given one chance by Rainwin. If he could control his abilities, he could live in the city. If not; he had to leave and never come back."

"What happened?" I asked, wondering what anyone could possibly do to upset Rainwin so much that he would make him or her leave forever. Leave … "Wait! He's alive?"

Carõ shrugged rather unconcernedly. "He could be."

My head buzzed as I tried to comprehend what he was saying until I got angry. "You didn't tell me!" I said, almost getting as angry as before. "You knew all this time, and you didn't tell me!"

"Would you have wanted to know?"

"*Yes!*" I said too quickly and then changed my mind. "No … I don't know! I don't even understand what they are!"

"They're powerful, strong, unstoppable magicians," he said. "An angry Draes is like a spark on a dry field, terrifying and deadly. Rainwin had me kill all of them, Zye, except you and Father. After that battle, I realized why he banished Father. In any human battle I might lose two or three men on a bad day, but in two hours against three hundred Draes I watched four thousand of my men die. It's so easy for them to kill without thinking … without trying. That's why Shintie and I never told you; the Draes who want to live normal lives can't because they're too afraid they'll hurt people unintentionally."

"Was Father like that?" My voice was becoming testy again.

"No," he said flatly. "Zye, you can't become angry."

My blood boiled even higher. "*You're* making me angry, Carõ," I pointed out. "Did you notice that? You love making me angry! You have to have that control, Brother. You may be a general of soldiers, but you're not of me."

"In case you hadn't noticed, you are a soldier, Zyemen," he rebounded.

"Don't call me that," I snarled. "And I'm not a soldier yet."

"Look down," Carõ said fiercely, "because I was almost positive that chain on your neck says 'soldier.' Or am I mistaken?"

My face was hot, and my fists were balled. The dog tag sitting under my shirt felt as if the little carved letters were pressing into my skin. I knew I shouldn't get angry, but it was becoming harder and harder to control myself with my brother.

"Realize your place, little brother," he said, smirking. "I am your general."

I snapped. Time inside the barn froze save for myself, and I pulled up my sword in both hands. Without even moving, I was inches from Carõ, my blade resting over his face. There was a look of surprise and shock but not fear in his expression. For some reason, the fact that he was my brother didn't register at that moment. The fact that no matter what he did I had to love him didn't occur to me. The only thing that did was everything he'd ever done wrong. Acting as my father, making me angry about being the youngest and smallest, always telling me to calm down … I wasn't calm now. I was so furious that I couldn't think straight. I swung my father's sword to the right and over and then stopped. Time unfroze, and my brother jumped out of the way of the sword that had just drawn blood. The rage that had possessed me a second earlier was gone, and the blade clattered loudly to the floor. I couldn't speak; I couldn't move. I just stared at the inch-long gash in Carõ's neck.

"When that sword tastes O' Maari's blood, don't curse my name," he said, sheathing his sword and not so much as pressing a hand to the bloody wound.

"Carõ—" I could barely talk. I couldn't believe what I had just gotten so close to doing. "I'm sorry. I don't even know what I—"

"I know you don't," he cut me off. "Like I said, it's not a controllable power. Draes are dangerous; I should kill you now."

"But you won't?"

"Not while I can avoid it."

"Let me know something, Brother," I said, glancing down at my blade but not picking it up. "Should I fear you?"

"I'll give you this answer," he said and stooped to take my blade by the hilt. "I can kill you. I have the ability, you know that, but at the moment I don't have the necessity."

There was a long pause as Carõ turned my sword around to offer it back. Slowly, as if not wanting to touch it, I wrapped my sweaty fingers around the metal.

"Thanks," I said in an undertone, sheathing my sword without looking down.

"Zye, can you honor one thing, now that you know?" Carõ asked.

I waited.

"Don't tell anyone you're a Draes; Shintie and I were careful to keep it a secret for sixteen years. It would be a shame to see that disappear for nothing so you wouldn't disappoint someone."

"Are you talking about O' Maari?"

"Yes."

I was going to retort but decided to bite my tongue. "I was going to meet her at the woods for a fire before we both leave tomorrow."

Carõ sighed. "Why don't you go and forget this for a while. The next time you see me you'll be a fully trained soldier and ready to be a Draes."

"Are you sure it wouldn't be better to kill me now?" I asked. I didn't want to die by any means, but if it was going to happen eventually, I'd rather have my brother do it.

Carõ's answer was pretty much what I had expected, though. "No," he said.

I turned to get Starra from her stall. Then one final thought came to me. "Carõ?" I turned my head to see that he had started to leave but then stopped. "How do you kill a Draes?"

There was a long pause, and I wondered if he even knew, but then he replied, "Only a creature stronger than a Draes can kill a Draes, and then only magically. Right now, the only known thing that meets that criterion is a dragon, and they're gone."

I fiddled absentmindedly with a small branch poking out of the dim campfire. It was night and dark and quiet, altogether quite peaceful. I was leaning against the damp bark of an old willow with O' Maari's head resting against my shoulder. We had camped in the immense forest of Hishe thousands of times before, starting when O' was only about five and

I was seven. Starra and Daren stood a few feet away, tethered loosely to an overhanging branch and nickering softly back and forth.

"Zye." O' Maari spoke after almost ten minutes of nothing but the two horses nickering and the constant crackling and popping of the flames. She glanced up at me. "Are you all right? You haven't really said much since we got here."

"Yeah," I said easily, straightening up a little. "I'm just tired."

"You're tired?" she asked, raising an eyebrow, "I know you better than that, Zye. What's wrong? Please. I won't tell anyone if you don't want me to."

I sighed heavily. I knew I could trust O' Maari with my life, and I knew she wouldn't tell anyone anything I didn't want to get out. Carõ had warned me not to tell even her, and maybe for once he could be right in that thick head of his. He had been right about getting too angry. But he had never said I couldn't tell her about my father.

"Um," I said slowly, licking my lips, "my father is a Draes."

"Oh," she breathed, obviously not expecting that. "But I thought Carõ led the Hishe army against all of them. I thought they were all dead."

"My father was the last one; he didn't fight in that battle for or against them."

"Isn't that power passed down?" she asked "From father to son?"

"Yeah."

"If you don't mind me asking …" She paused.

I waited for a moment, but I knew she wasn't going to finish the sentence. When I couldn't keep quiet any longer, I lied. "I don't know, O'," I said. "When I asked Carõ, he was still unsure."

"Do you even know how bad of a liar you are?" she asked, lifting her head up so that she wasn't leaning any weight on me.

"Did you think I was lying?"

"I know you were lying." She looked at me. "I'm all right with you not wanting to tell me—it's your family—but I'm not all right with you lying."

"I do know," I said finally, sighing. "Carõ told me."

"Will you tell me?"

"Do you want to know?"

She thought for a moment. "Yes."

It took me a while to force myself to say it, to admit it, out loud. "Me."

O' Maari spend a minute trying to find a response. Finally, she said, "I thought so. That's why you were being so evasive. Does that mean you're the last one?"

"Yes, in Hishe, anyway," I said, leaning against the tree again. "But Carõ hinted that my father might still be alive."

"That would be incredible to meet him now. Are you going to look for him?"

"I don't know if he is alive, just that he could be," I pointed out. "And in any case he couldn't come back. Carõ was forced to kill all of them save for me. Plus, he probably isn't even on X48 anymore; there are thousands of planets that can support life."

"If you ever do, though, and you find him, just don't be mad at him," O' Maari said, resting her head on my shoulder again, "He might have left to protect his own life, but he was also protecting his family and his son's sanity."

"Carõ?" I asked, looking down at her.

"Yes," she said with slight surprise in her tone. "What kind of man would it turn him into if he had to kill his father and young brother?"

"Slightly more sane than he is now." I smiled, feeling tired.

O' Maari chuckled and closed her eyes. Before she fell asleep, though, I thought of something else.

"O'?"

"Yeah?"

"You're not afraid of me, are you?"

"Why, because you're a Draes?"

"Yes."

"No, you're not any different," she said sleepily. "Honestly, I can rest a little easier now, knowing you're hard to kill. You'll prove to be useful on the battlefield, I think."

Her loyalty at the moment wasn't relieving; it was annoying. It just seemed stupid. I had not three hours ago come within inches of killing a high general and my brother; it would be so much easier to kill a little girl. Carõ had warned me not to blame him when I hurt O' Maari, but I knew that wouldn't happen. She didn't make me angry like he did. In almost ten years of knowing her I could count on one hand the number of times we had argued angrily. But still, I couldn't get everything Carõ had said out of my mind. I was scared of myself now, scared of what I could do. I had frozen time and teleported without even trying or thinking. Powerful magicians weren't unheard of, but even Raymond Green couldn't stop time.

I glanced over at O' Maari, but she was sleeping quietly. I resigned myself to watching the dying flames and studying their ever-changing colors. I noticed how they ate away at the dead branches and leaves, leaving nothing but a layer of blackness behind. A Draes was like a fire, an angry demon that destroyed and killed everything and everyone in its path. One spark could set an entire field or city to flame; one flash of anger could cause a Draes to do the same thing. I was beginning to be too tired to think, and I knew that if I dwelled on it much longer I would have nightmares. My head leaned back against the tree trunk, and I was asleep not more than a minute later. Before I was completely asleep, though, I watched the glowing embers behind my eyelids.

The sun was low in the sky when I woke up the next morning, and the dim fire was nothing but ashy wood. O' Maari's head was resting lightly on my shoulder. I turned my head so that my cheek brushed against her velvety cocoa hair and watched her sleep for a moment.

"O'," I whispered softly, "I have to go."

She woke up immediately and looked up at me, her hair falling over her emerald-green eyes. She sat up straighter and pushed the thin locks from her smooth face. "What time is it?" she asked blurrily.

I pushed myself to my feet and scaled the tree we'd been sleeping against. The thick, dense branches made it easy to pull myself swiftly to the top. From there, about twenty feet up, I could see a large amount of the woods we were sitting in, some farms, and the distant wall. To the west sat a sliver of Red peaking over the Hishe wall, trying to provide light to the waking city. I couldn't see my house in particular, but I knew I was about an hour's ride away. I was an hour north of my house, meaning I had one hour of riding out of the way. I jumped from the tree and landed lightly on the balls of my feet. O' Maari was untying the horses from their makeshift post and sliding Daren's bit into his mouth.

"It's about six hours into the day," I said, placing a sheet and saddle on Starra's back and ducking under her barrel to grab the girth.

"You need to leave, don't you?" she asked, tacking her own horse.

"Yes, and I'm already cutting it close leaving a day before training starts."

"Can I at least have a good-bye?" she asked, shouldering her leather bag.

I smiled slightly and then realized that this was the last time I would see her for a year. I took a step forward and hugged her tightly, resting my chin on the top of her head for a moment. I hadn't until now thought about how much I would miss her.

"I'm going to miss you," she whispered, her voice muffled by the cloth of my shirt.

"Me too," I muttered. Then I grinned as a thought occurred to me. "Wow," I said, astonished, "when I see you again, you'll be fifteen."

She looked up at me. "And you'll be seventeen; almost of age."

Almost of age, I thought. *Wow, she's right, I am. Only two more years and I'll be eighteen.* "I'll … I'll see you later, O' Maari."

I backed up, pressed my lips to the back of her hand, and leapt easily into the saddle. I tapped the mare on the sides, and at once she took off in a full gallop. I didn't even need to tell her to jump when we met obstacles; she knew what she could barrel through and what she needed to cross. In the back of my mind I hoped that O' Maari hadn't noticed my face becoming hot when I left.

After a minute or two, Starra was able to escape the forest. Once we were on a paved road, she sped up without a cue. Everything around us became a blur of color. All the sounds of the early day—people talking on the side of the road, horses nickering loudly to each other, swordsmen challenging guards and soldiers to duels—faded into nothing. The only things that I could hear were the constant, steady pounding of Starra's hooves on the pavement and the light thrumming of my own and my horse's heart.

Starra was the kind of horse that would and could gallop for twelve hours straight without resting, eating, or even slowing down, but I wasn't *that* stupid. At about midday, after covering more than half the distance to the wall, we stopped at a small, shabby market. It was filled to capacity with farmers and hunters trading for everyday items and pleading with sellers to lower the offer. I had never in my life been to a trading market; my family was quite wealthy, and we had never had the need. I rode awkwardly into the market, hoping that someone would accept gold for food. I didn't have anything to trade.

It wasn't long before a young man in torn, filthy clothes and long, untamed jet-black hair and beard came up to me. "How much," he said, grinning evilly, "you want for your horse, here?"

"She's not for sale," I responded flatly. No human alive could take this horse away from me. "Please let me through."

The man moved to the side to let me pass but continued to follow easily next to Starra. "Anything you want," the man offered, patting my horse on the neck with a thick hand. "Anything you could imagine."

"I told you," I said, cueing Starra to kick the man in the back of the legs. She did, and he fell headfirst into a muddy puddle. He was unharmed but red with anger. "Nothing will separate me from this horse."

I patted her on the neck and continued into the market, more careful about who got near us. Several other traders offered me food and money for anything valuable I carried: my sword, my gold, my tack, Starra, and anything else that they liked the looks of. Finally, after almost half an hour of inching through the trading market and refusing offer after offer, I found what looked like a small food stand. A young woman stood before several rows of fruit, bread, and a large trough of crystal-clear water. She smiled at me when she saw me.

"Can I help you?" Her voice was sweet but automatic, as if she'd said the words a thousand times before.

"That depends." I grinned and dismounted. "Do you take gold, or do I have to trade you something? I need everything I have."

"Don't worry, soldier boy." She rolled her eyes and flipped a lock of hair from her face. "I'll take gold."

"Soldier boy?" I asked. "How did you know I'm a soldier?"

The woman laughed. "You're not the first teenager to ride a war horse through the market today like you have no idea where you are."

"We're that obvious, are we?" I asked.

She chuckled softly, "The rich ones are; I saw you fending off the horse traders." She glanced at Starra. "She's beautiful, by the way."

"Thank you." I paused. "Could I have a drink of water?"

"Help yourself. It's one piece of silver."

I dug through my bag for a moment, trying and failing to find silver. "Here." I gave up and handed her a piece of gold. "Just keep it."

The woman laughed at me. "I wish you soldiers would come through every day; none of you know what silver is," she added.

"Thanks," I said. I slid the bit from Starra's mouth and watched her drink deeply for a moment. Then she backed up a step to allow me in. I took a short drink of the cool water and splashed some on my face. Also, I bought some apples and bread for later on and packed away the food and remaining money. Finally, I placed the bit back into Starra's mouth and stuck my foot in the left iron.

I pulled myself back into the saddle and turned to face the young woman. "Thanks."

She smiled back. "Good luck."

I nodded and kissed softly to Starra. She trotted back toward the road, unable to canter in the crowd, and nickered warningly whenever someone got in her way. When we reached the road again, I tapped her sides, and she bolted off. She reached a full gallop in seconds, and I allowed my mind to wander. I knew Starra could find the city gates by herself in a nice amount of time even though I hadn't ever ridden there myself. Carõ had taken her on the route once with Mayan just for this reason; he knew that my mind liked to wander when I was riding.

With some difficulty, I turned my attention back to the road and clicked to Starra to pick it up; she had in the last few minutes slowed to a canter, "Come on, Starra," I said, tapping her on the sides with my feet. "Let's go! Gallop!"

The cue had the opposite effect, however; it was like setting off a bomb. Starra shot up on her hind legs, spun wildly and frantically when she landed, and reared high again. She landed the second time heavily and took off in a dead bolt. I pulled desperately at the reins, but the stupid reaction only sent her higher. I jammed my left heel in her side and pulled the reins to the right in both hands, forcing her to spin in tiny circles. I continued to turn her until she calmed down, glancing up every so often to make sure we weren't about to hit anyone.

"*Starra,*" I said when she was still and we were both breathless. "What was that about?"

Underneath me, the mare was a stiff iron bar; every nerve and muscle was taut with anxiety. I glanced around. The road was suddenly, strangely empty; no one and nothing was in sight. I was totally alone in a narrow alley.

Then, it happened again. Starra reared again, almost flipping over, and something huge and black darted past us. It was horse-sized, that I was sure of, and moving at about horse speed. But it was blurry, as if with magic. It was just a black streak as it shot past us again. I ducked quickly as it did, sliding sideways and almost out of the saddle, for the rider had been brandishing a sword at just my height. I took out my own blade and waited for the horse and rider to return. When they did, they stopped.

The horse seemed to have no acceleration; it simply stopped perfectly, like something colliding with a wall. He was tall, at least a hand over Starra, and jet black, with no markings whatsoever. His rider was my age. He was thin, with a pointed face, golden-blond hair, and blue eyes.

"Jumpy mare you've got there," he said with a laugh and added sarcastically, "she'll make a great war horse."

"Most horses aren't accustomed to having swords thrown at them," I pointed out, even though I knew that war horses should be.

"Fire Rain is." The boy patted the horse on the side and sheathed his sword. "I'm Jonathan, by the way," he added. "Jonah for short. I'm also a soldier in training."

"Zye." I reached over to shake his hand. "If you're in the same position as me, then why did you attack me?"

"I wasn't actually going to hit you," Jonah said, laughing, "Or your beautiful mare." He nodded at Starra. "I just wanted to see what you two could do under pressure. I bid your mare good luck in a real war, with people who *do* want to kill her."

"She's normally pretty calm," I said, turning her to follow Jonah toward the gate, which was still about two hours away. "I think she's just tired; I live in Center End, and we left this morning."

Jonah just stared at me incredulously. "Center End is two hours away on a riding star," he said. "How on X48 did you ride a horse that distance in a day?"

"She's a fast horse." I shrugged.

"I don't doubt it." He laughed. "So, in twelve hours, you rode from the middle of the city to the main gates? Wow, you're some rider!"

"Thank you." We began to canter, moving quickly enough to finish the trip before dark but slowly enough to still talk. "So how long have you been up here?"

"A few days," Jonah said. "I live on South End, so I left about two weeks ago."

I nodded; it was a reasonable time for an average horse. The city was divided into five parts: Center End, South End, East End, West End, and North End. All but Center End had a huge gate to enter and exit the city, and the gate at North End was the largest and most heavily guarded. It was where Hishe armies left for battle and, if it should ever actually happen, where another city would probably attack us. Intertwined with the five sections were several natural features. The most impressive was the forty-thousand-square-mile forest called Shade Under that separated Center from North. It was the largest forest in Hishe and full of thousands of animals and birds for hunting. Every domestic animal found in the city could probably also be found in Shade Under, even horses. Besides the forest, there was a lake between West and South that was several hundred miles wide and a hundred and twenty miles deep; again, it was the largest of its kind on the entire planet. It was mainly used for fishing and aquatic farming, but some was sectioned off for swimming. I had been there only once on a class trip with the others in my age group. I could still remember how immense the lake was, stretching farther than I could see over the planet. Apart from some much smaller woods and ponds, the rest of Hishe was just a big black desert with dramatically different seasons. Most of X48, in fact, is covered in thin jet-black sand, with no grass or soil anywhere.

After riding for a while, we reached a large, open training field covered with hundreds of horses and riders. There were probably five hundred sixteen-year-olds riding around or talking to each other, all with swords and horses.

"How many kids are in training?" I asked, staring around.

Jonah grinned at my expression. "Seven hundred, I think."

"Seven *hundred*."

"Well." Jonah's smile faded. "What did you think, thirty? Hishe's a big place; we need all the protection we can get."

Before I could respond, however, a horn sounded over the field. It sounded like a trumpet: one long note, sharp and clear, held for over a minute. As if responding to the horn, all seven hundred soldiers in training, even those just arriving, began to form a great row over a half mile long.

I glanced over at Jonah, and he nodded back. The nod said, *follow me.* We cantered over to one end of the line, which was still forming quickly, and I whispered for Starra to stay perfectly still. Most of the horses that I could see were quite calm and patient. I couldn't see any of them acting up or rearing or spinning or anyone falling off.

"What are we doing?" I asked, not daring to look over at Jonah as two men came riding past the line at steady lopes. It was rare to see someone riding in western style.

"Shhh," Jonah hissed. Fire Rain threw his head as if agreeing with him.

I watched the two men loping slowly past each teen, sometimes stopping to ask questions. They didn't seem to be too nice; whenever they stopped by someone, they got as close as possible on horseback. As they approached us, I felt my hands clench tightly over the reins and become instantly hot and sweaty.

"Jaylan's brother," said one of the men laughingly when he reached us. Somehow, he was only a few inches from Jonah's face despite the fact that both were on horses. "I'm going to have fun with you. I'm ..." But he stopped abruptly when he saw me. So did the other man.

"Well, well." He grinned. "Who do we have here?"

"Little brother of the great war hero, Carõ." The other laughed and turned to face both Jonah and me. "Listen, you two, I don't want anyone thinking they're smarter than they are. We rule this training ground; we have for thirty-eight years. We trained Carõ, Jaylan, and Shintie; we can and will train you two into perfect fighters."

The first man turned to face the rest of the crowd. Then he loped back to center and spook in a booming voice. "I don't want any goofing off from any of you," he shouted. "I am the ruler here, and you will do as I say when I say it. Some of you might have expected special treatment because of the fact that your brothers and fathers are well known in the Hishe armies. I am sorry to tell you all this, but you're wrong. Everyone is treated the same here; no one is hated or loved, feared or respected. No one is put up on a high throne to watch everyone else fight. Am I clear?"

There was a smattering of consent. Some nodded, and others said something like, "Yes," or "Yes, sir." Anger crossed the man's face.

"I said," he hollered, his face turning red, "*Am I clear?*"

At once, all seven hundred teenagers responded in a resounding unison, "Yes, sir."

At the sudden shouting, some of the horses threw their heads or shifted in place. It seemed, though, that no one fell off.

The man smiled under the dark hair hanging in his face. "Good," he said. "Here's another thing: this"—he paused to hold up the horn he had blown a few minutes ago— "is a War Caller's Horn. Any time I want your attention, I will use this. When a battle ends, a general will use this to tell his soldiers. This little trumpet is going to be your lifeline for the next year, so you'd better drop what you're doing and listen when you hear it. If not, there will be consequences. Am I clear?"

"Yes, sir," responded the soldiers loudly.

"See," the man said to his fellow, "they learn quickly. Your turn."

The second man nodded and turned his horse to face us. "Now," he said. His voice was also magnified somehow. "I want two even groups: one over to the east with Kylen and the others with me. Split now, but I warn you: you can choose to be with friends, but you'll pay for the mistake later."

"Jaylan is your brother?" I asked Jonah as we rode over to Kylen's group.

"Yeah," he answered, shrugging, "and a rotten showoff too. He thinks he's the best soldier out there. Well, besides Shintie he's probably right. I can't believe your brothers are Shintie and Carõ."

I rolled my eyes. "You and everyone else."

Jonah looked at me sideways. "What's that mean?" he asked.

"Very few people can believe that my brother is Carõ, the great war hero. In most people's eyes, I'm just a young, scrawny teenager who will never live up to his brothers."

"According to Jaylan, as a soldier there's not much to live up to for Carõ."

"For Shintie there is," I started, but I was interrupted when Kylen suddenly blew the war horn again. I could see some of the soldiers nearest to Kylen clap their hands over their ears from the loud blast.

"*Attention!*" he shouted, "Follow me, and try to keep up because we won't wait for you. Also, training starts now. I will lead, and I want all of you side by side in a straight line like you were earlier. If I see one of you break the line or curve it, we will come back to Hishe and begin the trip again!"

Eyes wide, I glanced over at Jonah. "How far from Hishe is Silver?"

"Longer than it would be reasonable to turn back from and start over," he said, glaring at the trainer.

"Do you honestly believe he would do that?"

"I don't entirely want to find out."

I laughed, and we found a spot in line near the left end. Kylen spurred his horse into a gait faster than what I knew to be western and arched in a wide half circle. He galloped along the line as before but not stopping, only gaining speed. When he reached the end, he arched left and started side passing to be in the middle, still at a gallop. Once there, he straightened out and headed forward. All of the teenagers in line looked sideways at each other. Everyone was too afraid to start first and break the formation.

Kylen was quickly gaining distance as we stood motionless. We'd have to go eventually, but leaving meant starting. Whoever got the few hundred kids going at the same time was probably going to end up being some kind of leader. The last thing I wanted to do was make myself a general like my glorified brother, but I didn't really have another choice. I tried to remember how Shintie had told me he started advances. I thought for a moment, making sure I was remembering correctly, and turned to Jonah.

"We'll start a gallop at one," I said. "Count from five as loud as your voice allows, and the sound will travel over the line."

"Will that work?" he asked, still watching the disappearing soldier trainer.

"My brother said it's a good way to try, at least." I shrugged.

"Go for it."

"*Start on one!*" I shouted, throwing my head back and using magic to enhance the sound. "Five!"

The teenagers within earshot looked over and realized what I was doing.

"Four!" I was joined in the second number by probably twenty or so on either side of us.

"Three!" I almost didn't hear my voice that time because almost half of the teenagers said it with me.

"Two!" I was sure we had at least three-quarters of the several hundred.

"One!" Every single soldier in training screamed the final number. I couldn't hear my voice, Jonah's, or that of the boy to my other side. When the single syllable had finished, three hundred and fifty horses were spurred forward. I clicked to Starra to not run as fast as I knew she could so that the other riders could keep pace. By the end of a long minute, we were all galloping in one perfect line, each looking side to side constantly to check that we weren't too far forward or back. I glanced at Jonah; he was throwing his head back with laughter.

"Is something amusing?" I asked.

"The simple fact that this worked." He chuckled.

"Were you expecting it not to?"

"No," he said. "I did not expect three hundred–some kids to take off on horses all at once and not leave someone walking. It's a good thing Carō taught you that."

"Actually, he didn't," I said. "Shintie did."

"Ah," he nodded, not laughing so hard anymore but still in a good mood. "I would assume a soldier has more ground experience than a general."

"That sounded as if it meant something," I said pointedly.

Jonah shrugged. "I just mean that someone who actually does that fighting would know how to lead an advance better than someone who sits behind the scenes. I know generals have a lot to do," he added, quickly seeing the anger on my face, "but they're not actually, physically fighting for their lives like we will be."

I pressed my lips together and for a while said nothing.

"You don't want to be a general, correct?" Jonah asked, breaking the silence.

"No." I had decided that a long time ago. "No way in hell would I be a general."

"Good." Jonah laughed again. "I'm glad you're not like your brother. Jaylan and Carõ may be good friends, but my brother hates yours for being a general."

"Isn't Jaylan Carõ's second-in-command?" I asked.

"Yeah, but he fights," Jonah pointed out.

"I don't like it either," I admitted unwillingly.

Shintie and I fought for Hishe. Carõ leaned over a map and told us who should die where.

5

CHAPTER FIVE

I felt as if I were about to fall off Starra's back. It was near midnight on the third day of straight riding. We stopped early each morning for a short rest, mainly for the horses. Afterward, Kylen would allow us to ride in a group rather than a line. When night fell completely after each day, the trainer would yell for us to form a line again for safety reasons.

Most of the time, we didn't talk. Sometimes, I would hear the occasional snippet of wary conversation, but for the most part it was silent. Silent, that is, save for the pounding of 350 sets of horses' hooves against the black sand.

At the moment, I was cantering steadily beside Jonah but couldn't see him. It was pitch black everywhere, and there was no chance of seeing Kylen, who was probably a mile in front of us by now. The only hint that there was someone to my left was the barely visible silhouette of Fire Rain's neck bobbing up and down. Other than that, I couldn't see anything. I wasn't used to this kind of darkness. I had never even left my city; now I was almost five hundred miles away from it. Even at this time of night, in the absence of a planet moon like Earth, Hishe was never this black. The pure nothingness of what I could see was almost intimidating. It didn't really surprise me, then, that when the war horn suddenly blasted from not far off, I about jumped out of my saddle.

"You'd think I'd be used to that by now," I heard Jonah say, his voice groggy from lack of sleep, "but that thing gives me a heart attack every time he uses it."

"*Attention!*" came Kylen's voice, magnified to reach everyone in the group. "We're resting here for the night! You have until dawn to sleep."

Jonah and I slowed to a trot and rode over to a spot outside the majority of the rest of the group. I covered my mouth with the back of my hand and didn't even try to stifle a yawn. Beside me, Jonah had dismounted and was pouring something in the sand. A moment later, there was the sound of something being struck across wood, and fire was created. Jonah had formed a small bowl in the sand and filled it with a thick, clear liquid that was apparently very flammable. The fire was small but white hot and provided a good amount of light. I pulled my cramped right leg over Starra's back and nearly fell over trying to get my left out of the iron. I patted Starra on the neck and slid the bit from her mouth. As soon as she was free of the metal, she lay down with a heavy snort.

Jonah laughed. "I think she's tired," he said, untacking Fire Rain.

I finished removing the mare's saddle and sat next to her, leaning most of my weight against her side. "Well, that would make two of us." I shrugged, unbuckling my sword and sheath from my belt. "I'm exhausted."

Jonah sank down to the sandy ground, like me, leaning heavily against his horse, whom he had to cue to lie down. "One more day," he said happily, removing a thick sheath from his back. It was the first time I had realized that he kept his sword on his back and not on his belt like most. "One more day of riding, anyway."

I rolled my eyes. "Yeah," I agreed. "Then we have to fight each other for a year."

Jonah gave a huge, lionlike yawn and folded his hands behind his head. "That's not today," he reminded me. "That's tomorrow. We need to sleep now and worry about a fake war tomorrow."

"What is that, by the way?" I asked, watching the flames dance on the water-like substance.

"What, the oil?" He gestured at what I was watching and I nodded. "Haven't you ever used oil before?"

"No. What is it?" I said. "Enchanted water?"

Jonah laughed. "No, it's natural. It comes from underground or something. It's my father's occupation to collect it, so most of the time it's free."

"Do you drink it?"

He shook his head and continued laughing. "I wouldn't suggest it. You burn it; it provides light. How does your house have light?"

"With fire, but with magic." I shrugged. "I know you have to feed some fires, but I didn't know you could start one on your own."

Jonah tossed me a small box with sandpaper-like covering. Inside were a handful of short sticks dipped in black powder. "Drag the black end over the outside of the box," instructed Jonah.

I did, and the little stick of wood burst into life. With surprise at being so close to the flame, I yelled and dropped it. A few seconds after it landed, it went out. Jonah laughed again, and I threw the box back to him. He replaced it in a bag on his saddle and leaned back against Fire Rain's side. After some time, his eyes slid closed, and his breathing became slow and steady. I wished I could do the same, but I had never been able to just fall asleep. My mind gave me unsettling visions that became similarly unsettling dreams. When Red started peeking over the horizon, I was not only tired but also paranoid.

About the same time I noticed the sun, the war horn sounded in a hard, drawn-out note that swept across the field. I jerked fully awake, and my head cracked loudly against something icy cold and solid. It took me a few seconds to realize that, during the night, I had slid to the side and was now laying sideways next to Starra. My head had landed on a metal stirrup; my ear had folded back on itself, and I could feel something wet and warm there.

I pushed myself to my feet and felt the back of my ear to find a small gash and a bit of blood. A cut on my ear was nothing compared to what Shintie came home with sometimes, the worst of which being … never mind.

I watched the rising sun as I tacked Starra. The horizon looked unfamiliar. It spiked up at random, uneven spots as if the ground were raised up. I glanced over at Jonah, who was blurrily strapping his jet-black saddle to Fire Rain's back. "Jonah," I asked, climbing easily into my saddle, "there aren't mountains on X48, are there?"

"Well, yeah." He shrugged, pulling his golden hair back with a strip of leather. "Mainly only that range you can see off in the distance."

He pointed at the raised land. "There's a few nice-sized ranges scattered throughout X."

I nodded. For some reason, the fact that there were real mountain ranges on X48 surprised me. I had learned all my life that our planet was just a flat, barren desert land with very few variations anywhere. I knew that Silver was an exception, but it just seemed odd that there was so much I didn't know about my own planet. I hoped Jonah wouldn't start calling me a rich man's son like some kids had when I was younger.

For the rest of the trip, I shut up about the stupid questions. We rode at a steady pace until about midday, when Kylen stopped us suddenly.

We were standing before a wide field of what appeared to be thick fog. The trainer waited until all of us were stopped and in earshot before speaking.

"Welcome to the Silver Canyon," he said. "This will be your new home for the next year. There are only two laws that I will give you, and the rest is up to you: one, no one sits out of a fight, and two, no one is permitted to kill. Am I understood?"

There was a general murmur of consent, and Kylen's expression become one that Carõ would give me when he looked down at me with particular loathing. "Good luck, the lot of you," he sneered. Then he threw his war horn at us. It arched high and fell toward Jonah and me. I made the mistake of reaching up and catching the heavy, almost metallic cone. Then, without another word, the trainer turned his horse and galloped along the fog bank.

I turned to Jonah. "Is it always hidden in fog?" I asked, assuming the canyon lay beneath, "How on X48 are we supposed to get down?"

"I have a better question," said Jonah, staring worriedly at the fog. "How are we even supposed to *see*?"

I thought about that for a moment, but it didn't concern me. I blinked once, and the fog vanished. I guess "vanished" is a bad word to use, because it was still there; I just couldn't see it anymore. I have the ability to magnify my vision by hundreds of thousands of millions of times. Now, I realized, that is an ability specific to being a Draes. But I could easily see below the thick smog. There were hundreds of small ledges jutting out from the canyon wall that were several feet thick. They seemed thick enough to support a horse and rider. I realized that our only way of getting down would be to use the ledges as stairs.

I grinned to myself and blinked to restore my vision back to normal. "I have an idea of how to reach the bottom of Silver," I shouted over the three hundred teenagers. At once, they stopped riding around and talking to look up at Jonah and me.

"There are plenty of ledges coming out from the wall; they're thick enough to hold you. From what I can see, there is about thirty feet of fog at the top, so stick close to someone. After that, your visibility shouldn't be affected. I'll blow the war horn if something bad happens."

As I had expected, there was an angry outburst of shouting, laughter, and jeering. I knew the other teenagers had absolutely no reason to trust my word alone. Honestly, had the roles been reversed, I probably wouldn't believe someone telling me that he could see through thirty feet of silvery-gray fog.

"*Hey!*" I shouted over the mocking retorts. "If you want to sit here and vote or something, that's fine with me, but we *need* to get to the bottom of Silver. After a while, we're going to need someone to lead us, and I'm not saying I want to be that someone; actually, I'd rather not, but we do need order. Whether you follow me down Silver or not is your choice, but that's the only way I can think of to get down, so I'm going. Also, remember something: we are soldiers now! Our lives are not supposed to be easy and safe."

Without so much as a backward glance toward Jonah, I dug my heels into Starra's sides, and she sprang forward. I cued her to jump as she reached the ledge of the canyon, and I felt her powerful back legs launch us from the solid ground. We fell through the empty air for about ten feet until she landed lightly on the first ledge. It had to be a lot more solid than I had anticipated, because it didn't groan or crack under our weight at all. Starra was still tired (as was I) from traveling so far, and I paused for a moment to allow her to rest. However, I had little time to stop because a moment later, I heard a loud, ominous crack. I spurred the mare into another frantic gallop and blinked to fix my vision. As the fog disappeared, another ledge came into view. Then came another and another. About halfway down, I blinked again. The fog had long since passed away, but I had kept my advanced vision just to be able to foresee any oncoming problems.

I heard something behind me. At first, I didn't know what it was, but a moment later, I did. It was the unmistakable thunder of hooves against solid rock, and I had a good idea of who it was.

Moving at her top speed, Starra took a little over an hour to reach the bottom of the wall. By that time, Jonah and Fire Rain weren't the only ones following us. As my exhausted mare found flat ground, I watched hundreds of horses pounding down the wall. Each one appeared from nowhere out of the bottom of the fog bank. The shrill whinnies of the soldier's' mounts whenever one lost its footing or got in another's way became one continuous scream as they bolted down the canyon side.

There was a flash of blurred blackness that meant Jonah and Fire Rain were the first of the group to reach level land. I made a mental note to ask him why his horse didn't have any acceleration and looked like a blur when moving at a speed half of what Starra could do. Even as the horse slowed to a trot, his legs and head arched as if he were barely moving.

"That was amazing!" Jonah said happily, stopping easily for his horse's fox-trot next to me. "How'd you think of doing that?"

"I don't know." I shrugged, looking around. "It just kind of came to me. It wasn't like we were about to get an elevator."

Jonah threw back his head and laughed. "You really are Shintie's little brother."

For some reason, that made me grin quite genially. For the first time, I wasn't being compared to Carō.

6 CHAPTER SIX

The next three days were full of fast-paced confusion. Kylen, it seemed, had given us as little information as possible before leaving and wasn't coming back anytime soon. Thanks to Jonah, I had become the high general of my side, but he was second-in-command as payback. The soldiers on the other side had chosen their two generals as well. They had sent a letter to Jonah and me the very next day after arriving in Silver, but I couldn't remember their names. By the sound of it, they had scaled the wall about the same way we had, riding their horses down, but moving more slowly and with the aid of magic. Jonah had written back with a similar context, introducing us and offering a truce of three days before any attacks. They consented. Right away, Jonah and I had started the soldiers on setting up camps, clearing away trees, and familiarizing themselves with the land and with their swords, for those who had never picked one up in their life.

Presently, the two of us were sitting at a makeshift table in a planning shelter. The planning shelter was really no more than a small, out-of-the-way patch of grassy land covered by a thick cloth. We were poring over an old map of Silver that told us about where we were and where the "enemy" camp was. Overall, the canyon was a huge, thin slit in the planet with small patches of river and trees. Our own camp was stationed right next to one of these patches: a deep lake that touched both sides of the canyon walls and provided some protection. There was also a thin line of trees, maybe a quarter mile wide at most, pinning us against the western wall and lakeshore.

"See, look," Jonah was saying, tracing two hunks of land with his finger. The first was a small one about fifty miles from our camp and in between us and our lake blockade; the second was much larger and, it appeared, about equidistant from both camps. "Those are probably our best bet to attack. They're the biggest clear spots of land between us and them. Here"—he drew a line from the spot marking our camp, around to the opposite wall, and against the wall and lakeshore to the large clear land plot—"we can sneak around and prevent any Scarlets from sneaking around the other side." ("Scarlet" was the name of the opposing army; we were the Ambers.)

I nodded slowly, trying to think. "We don't even know how far away the eastern wall is, not to mention how deep that lake is. The horses can't swim that far, and by the looks of the map, there isn't going to be much room to walk on the land."

"Easy fix." Jonah smiled. He really seemed to be a natural leader; maybe he should have been the high general instead of me. "Maorin!"

There was a moment of silence before a tall, black-haired teenager loped easily into the planning shelter. He was thin with dark tan skin almost the color of the light brown sand that lay in Silver; in other words, he was almost impossible to see when galloping on his own horse, a solid dun.

Before he stepped through the tent, I hadn't heard any previous footfalls. Apparently neither had Jonah, because he asked, "Maorin, do you just walk silently, or were you eavesdropping on us?"

"Eavesdropping, sir," admitted Maorin. "But how can I help you?"

Jonah shook his head with slight amusement but motioned Maorin over. He pointed to the tiny dot that was our camp. "Ride, please, to the edge of this lake." He traced the line with his finger. "I want to know how far it is and how much space there is between the water's edge and the eastern wall. If there isn't enough room to canter two horses at a time down it, try to find another way across. Do you understand?"

"Yes, sir." Maorin nodded and trotted off.

"If this proves logical," Jonah continued, taking back my attention, "we can station archers at the back, maybe higher than everyone else, then magic fighters, and the cavalry at the front. How does that sound?" He paused, awaiting my answer. "Zye? Zye!"

I shook my head violently and looked up at Jonah, who had a slightly annoyed expression on his face. "Sorry, Jonah," I muttered, running a hand through my hair.

"You okay?" The stony look softened.

I stood up. Everything in the shelter was spinning slightly. "Air must have difficulty making its way to Silver's core. I'll be back in a few minutes."

I didn't wait for Jonah's response; I just walked as fast as I could into the open air. It was still thin and difficult to fill my lungs all the way, but it was more than I had been getting a moment ago. However, without the protection of the cloth overhead, Red's fiery heat had no problem burning my skin. It seemed that the dull sun was hotter than normal—that, or I was going as crazy as Carõ. He also hated the heat. I grabbed a tin of water off my belt and downed almost all of it, pouring a good amount over my head. I enjoyed the momentary relief until the sunlight dried it and burned the back of my neck with renewed vengeance.

Pain is a strange thing, I thought, heading to a well to refill my tin. *Of all the times I've fallen off a horse or cut myself or inhaled too much water, I have never felt anything like burns. Burns must be the worst possible kind of pain. I resolve to pity those burned by flames.* As I walked, I wondered if people on Earth had a sun as brilliant as Red. Was their source of light and life strong enough to burn their skin? We were supposed to be stronger than the people on Earth, but how was that even possible when the man who had advanced X48 into cities and civilization was from Earth? I forced myself not to think of Raymond Green as a strong man. I simply shuddered at the thought and wiped the sweat from the back of my neck.

As I walked around, I saw a large number of teenagers circling something that appeared to take up a lot of space. I edged myself up to the front to look inside the ring at what they were all watching. There were two kids. One was tall and thin, with a hunting spear, and the other was stockier and stronger, with hook swords in both hands. They were facing each other, ready to attack, and I wondered how long this year was going to last if after one day the soldiers were already at each other's throats. I was about to push through to stop them when I looked at their faces more closely. They were grinning. The taller one was laughing. When they ran forward to fight, it wasn't angry or violent; it was sport. The soldiers were playing! I calmed down a little and watched. Each was quite skilled with a familiar weapon, and the other teenagers got bored quickly.

"Switch weapons!" yelled someone near the front of the ring.

"No," somebody else called. "Have 'em fight Zye!"

At once, all the kids turned to look at me. Earlier that day, Jonah and I had been practicing with swords and had about killed each other. I was fast and agile with my attacks, but Jonah was stronger than anyone I'd ever met. He wasn't little, but he wasn't very muscular either, so I had readied myself for speed. When he came barreling at me with his sword high, I became angry, not at him but myself. I was angry that I had taken what little I knew about a soldier and prepared to fight him in only one way. Of course, I had switched tactics and fought him as I would Shintie, but my style was still different. It was first time I had fought since I had learned that I was Draes (not including my real fight with Carõ in the horse barn), but I think it changed something. Every move I made and step I took was angrier than ever before, more violent. I remembered wanting to really kill my brother a few days ago. The feeling I'd had this morning wasn't so strong, but it was similar.

Back in the ring of teenagers, I was being beckoned to the front. I guess when they had seen Jonah and me practicing earlier, they had taken the strange anger in my moves to be incredible skill. Now, every one of the Ambers, save for myself and Jonah, thought I was the best swordsman in the camp. If I was going to be the general, I at least wanted to be a general who was known for sword skill as well as leading.

I sighed with a laugh and gave in. "All right," I said, and the pleas to watch me fight went silent. "All right, I'll have a go at them."

The onlookers cheered happily, and the two boys I was approaching grew cocky grins. From what I heard as I entered the ring of people, they had been deemed the two best fighters in the camp not including me.

"All right," I said, more to the two soldiers then the surrounding hundreds. "First off, I'm a proper swordsman. What are your names?"

The two kids glanced at each other as if they'd never heard of introducing themselves before a fight.

I pursed my lips dryly. "I know you're not going to have the chance to do this in a real war, but for now I would appreciate it if you fought as if you had an ounce of some civility."

"Fight with civility?!" said the boy with the hook swords, laughing. "Of the crazy things you've said in the past two days, Zye ..."

He was cut off by the other kid, who pointed out, "Those crazy things have gotten us pretty far, Iren. I would listen to him." He stepped up to me and offered a free hand. "I'm Henner."

"Zyemen." I shook his hand, his fingers wrapped tightly around mine, and waited for the other.

Grumbling about the ridiculousness of it, he stepped forward, held the swords in one hand, and grasped mine in a deadly vice with the other. When we were both sure the blood flow in my hand had stopped, he let go and said roughly, "Iren."

The three of us stepped back to form a wide triangle and prepared for the fight. Henner twisted the spear around his hand and then caught it in one tight grip. Iren threw up one of the hook swords, caught the rounded end on the rounded end of the other, and spun it dangerously. I drew my own blade with a metallic slice as it passed over the sheath.

"Wait." Henner suddenly grinned. "Iren, give me your tiger hooks. Zye, give Iren your sword, and I'll give you my spear. This will be interesting."

I handed off my blade to Iren, who wrapped his thick fingers around it clumsily, and caught the shaft of Henner's spear when he threw it to me.

"Easy with that blade," I warned Iren as he swung it about wildly and realized it had a lot more weight than two thin tiger hooks. "It was my father's."

"It's a piece of metal to kill people with," said the stocky teenager coolly. "I'm not sentimental about my hooks."

"Come on, you two," Henner said excitedly. "Girls fight with words; let's see how much talent we have with a weapon we've never seen before."

A crooked grin pasted itself over my lips, and I took a firm grip on the wood beneath my fingers. The surface was smooth and light brown in color, and the weapon was much lighter than a sword. I had, however, no idea how to fight with it. The staff was at least six feet long, and the pitch-black metal blade on the end was well over a half foot to the point. I'd seen a city hunter only once in my life, and the spear he carried looked nothing like this. What I held was not a hunting tool; it was a deadly weapon.

I took a step forward, and at the exact same time so did Henner and Iren. Henner held the hook swords up awkwardly, and I jumped forward and threw the spear with a strong arm. With obvious experience deflecting spears, Henner leaned calmly to the side and missed my shot by a few inches. Iren ran forward, eager to attack me once I was disarmed, but I jerked my arm around and balled my hand into a fist. The spear flew back to my grip. I held up the staff in front of my face with both hands just in time to block Iren's swing with my sword. I felt the heavy blade slam against the wood, inches from my face, and the ends vibrated violently with the force. Amazingly, however, it didn't slice through the wood. My war-class flat sword didn't chop through a little stick. For about half a second, Iren and I stood there, frozen with the shock of what hadn't happened, and then I got my sense back about me. I jerked down my left hand and threw up my right, swinging the little stick forward to push back the sword. Once it wasn't close enough to hit me, I pulled my right hand back and pushed my left forward and down, slamming Iren in the chest with the shaft. The blow wasn't as strong as one with a sword hilt could be, but it was enough to force him backward and make him stumble on his heels for balance. Relying on the strength of the spear, I moved my hands to one side and swung it hard like a club. The staff collided with his side, and the second hit caused him to let go of my sword. I left him for a moment, so he could catch his breath and regain his weapon, and turned to Henner.

"Strong spear," I noted, sidestepping around him as I wondered how to fight against a weapon that, until yesterday, I hadn't even heard of.

"Thank you." Henner grinned. He was doing the same thing as me. "I can't help but notice your own strength in magic."

I shrugged to dismiss the unwanted compliment and took a quick step forward. He advanced in a strange sideways run, something probably perfected by his training in throwing spears, and held the hooks awkwardly together like one badly shaped sword. I could tell at once he wasn't at all accustomed to actual hand fighting; like the majority of spear-throwers and archers, he'd never had any practice. I twirled the shaft of Henner's weapon in one hand and flattened it to the underside of my arm so it became more like a one-handed sword. However, in the half second before I pushed my arm forward to slam against one of the hook swords, both us of stopped dead.

"You hear that?" Iren asked, recovered and serious.

Henner and I nodded slowly, and everyone become still and silent. Not one soldier blinked or moved a muscle; all of us strained our ears to find what most of us had missed. Jonah had come out of the tent, probably drawn out by the sudden lack of noise, and was standing near the front of the circle of boys.

Suddenly, it happened again. It was some kind of hissing, so faint it was almost inaudible. It lasted for a few seconds and was followed by a dull thud. Then all was still. The only movement among the group was a smaller, blond-headed boy suddenly muttering in a low undertone to another boy, who seemed to be his brother: "I'll bet you anything that's an arrow."

Jonah and I caught each other's gazes for a half second, and then he joined me in the ring. Henner handed Iren back his hooks, I gave Henner back his spear, and Iren tossed me my sword, which I caught easily. I knew the blond boy had to be right because he knew what he was talking about. He and his fellow both wore full arrow quivers over their backs and had short bows hanging off one shoulder; they were archers.

"It's not coming from Scarlet territory," said someone. "Who else is there?"

"The trainers?"

"They wouldn't shoot at us?"

"Maybe this is for real."

"Sandstiss soldiers?"

"It's a smart thought: kill off the kids before they turn into soldiers."

"*Quiet!*" hissed Jonah dangerously. "There are no soldiers to kill us! Remember, the lot of you *are* soldiers. You can't fear the same thing you're meant to become."

"Maybe the Scarlets are back on top of Silver," offered Henner, but he was cut off quickly by Iren.

"It's against the laws of the training grounds," he pointed out. "You can't leave to attack from above."

"There are no laws in war," Jonah said calmly. "However, if it would settle you, why don't you go see where the arrows are coming from and bring one back for an archer to inspect?"

Suddenly that idea became useless as another hiss echoed down, growing louder and louder until something short, thin, and jet black streaked in between Jonah and me.

7 CHAPTER SEVEN

Every boy in the ring stared in utter terror at the little streamline arrow imbedded in the sand. After a silent moment, the blond archer stepped forward, jerked the shaft free, and examined it. It was a nice arrow. I didn't know much about archery, but the few times I'd practiced it with Tayer, our arrows weren't nearly this perfect. It was about a foot and a half long, and the sharpened end was simply carved out of the wood rather than having a blade attached. The three feathers used to balance the shaft were long and unfamiliar. Two of them were black like the wood, but the third was pure white.

"If Sandstiss follows the same arrow code as us, which I think they do, this is a surrendering arrow," said the blond boy. "I'm guessing it took the archer a few tries just because of how deep we are. He must be pretty strong to send an arrow a good fifty miles straight down without it even slowing."

I turned to Jonah. "Why would someone send a sign of surrender without even fighting?"

He shrugged. "I don't know, but maybe we should go up there and check."

"It could be anyone," I said, sheathing my sword but keeping a hand tight on the hilt. "It could be a trap."

"God only knows until we find out," Jonah said roughly. Then he raised his voice to address more than only me, repeating his earlier words. "Remember, we're soldiers now; we can't wait for someone else to fight our battles. We are the men who fight and die with honor, not those who argue and live to be old cowards."

A cheer swelled around the group for a moment and died when I began to speak. "All right," I said, resisting the urge to draw my blade again. "Henner, Iren, you two are in charge until we return. Nothing should happen, as we still have today and tomorrow for peace, but if we're not back by then, send someone after us."

When Henner and Iren nodded in consent, Jonah shouted, "Now back to work!"

Once we were on our way to the wall and out of earshot of the others, I glanced at Jonah. "Any idea on how to get back out? The horses are still exhausted from yesterday, and they'll need all the energy they can get."

"For some reason you're the best magician I've seen," Jonah said, not looking at me, "which is strange for a soldier, but I'm not going to complain. I was thinking that if you are as powerful as you appear, you could manipulate a ledge in the wall to just elevate up to the top."

"I've never tried something like that, but I can," I said, wondering if that was even physically possible. "That reminds me, how do ride the way you do?"

"Come again?"

"Your horse," I said. "He has no acceleration, and he looked blurry when he wasn't even moving that fast."

"I'm not sure about the acceleration thing," he said, shrugging, "but ever since he was a colt, Fire Rain's looked blurry when he runs. I'm not complaining, though; my trainer said it makes him look faster than he really is."

It didn't take long to reach the wall. The planning shelter was situated directly beside it, and I hadn't traveled very far to reach the circle of soldiers. Looking up at the immense stone, I realized that I couldn't even begin to see the top. Still, Jonah's plan was worth a try. I focused on the rock in front of me and balled my right, relaxed hand into a quick fist. At once, a piece of rock, probably a foot thick, six feet long, and three or four feet wide, shot out at my command. I grinned to myself, thankful that it had worked, and the two of us stepped onto the ledge. I glared up with extended vision, watching the swirling fog and wondering how to continue.

"Do you know 'up' in Latin?" I asked.

Jonah frowned. "Is it not just 'sursus'?"

"Probably." I shrugged defensively. "But I'm bad with the language. I've never caught on."

"I would have assumed you to be fluent; you're such a powerful magician."

"I'm not a good magician because I can speak the language," I said and left it at that, unsure if I could trust Jonah not to spread the word of what I was.

I unclenched my hand and twisted it in a quick, upward circle. As my hand stopped near my shoulder, I said the Latin syllables in a harsh tone. O' Maari had always told me that I sounded angry when I spoke Latin, but the way of the language was so foreign to me that it was just unnatural to voice aloud. Unnatural or not, it worked. At the single word and twist of my hand, there was a loud crack. The ledge split from the wall and began sliding upward. I kept my hand where it was but turned my head up and willed us to pick up speed. Slowly but surely, we gained momentum until we were traveling at about the same pace as a galloping horse.

"This is better than climbing or riding," I heard Jonah say a few feet away, "but it's still going to take at least an hour if not more."

"Do you have a better idea?" I asked, not glancing at him.

"No," he said slowly. "I mean, riding stars would be too powerful, wouldn't they?"

"We'd end up burying the soldiers and more than likely all of Silver."

"This works, then." He retreated from the thought. "What is there that I could know about you, then?"

"What do you want to know?"

"If we have an hour's ride, we might as well try and become more knowledgeable about each other."

I considered him for a moment. Jonah was friendly, curious, and good natured, but was that enough to trust him? I decided to begin small. "I'm the youngest of four brothers: Shintie, Carõ, Tahll, and Rye. Rye, my twin, is a healer, but I've taught him to fence in our room."

This made Jonah laugh, "My cousin would envy your twin." He chuckled. "He's a teacher, and he's been dying for me to teach him to fight."

We both laughed for a moment and then fell silent for a few minutes. In that time, the only sound was the grinding of our ledge against the stone of the wall and the rush of air passing over us. It took Jonah a minute to realize that was all I was going to say. He began to speak himself. It turned out that Jonah was a middle child with an older brother, Jaylan, and a younger sister named Kira. Kira was less than a year old and not actually related to Jonah. For a reason unknown to him, his mother had left when he was ten, and, six years later, his father had taken in a little orphaned girl.

When he was finished, there was another uncomfortable silence, but this time it was joined with the feeling of Jonah's eyes sitting on my shoulder with immense weight.

"Is there something you want to voice?" I asked, only slightly irritated.

"I'm only marveling at your ability with magic," he explained innocently enough. "If you are a soldier and your brother is a healer, why isn't he the magician in the family and you the fighter?"

"I can fight," I protested, fearing what he was getting at.

"But you rely on magic like no one I know; you have that luxury that you're able to rely on magic. I'm only curious as to why."

There it was. Slowly, as if I were part of the rock we sped past, I answered his question, "Jonah, I can rely on magic so heavily because I'm not like the rest of you. I'm not a human; I'm a Draes."

There was another pause as I waited for Jonah to say something. It took him a while to come up with something pretty uncreative. "I thought they were all dead. Didn't your brother go up against an army of them?"

"Yes, all of them save for two: my father and me."

"He wasn't ordered to kill you?"

"He was ordered to kill the army. Rainwin knew about my father and me, so he tried to get around it, for Carõ's sake."

"Carõ's sake?"

"So he didn't have to kill his father and three-year-old brother."

"I understand." Jonah nodded. "And don't worry, I'm not going tell anyone what you are."

"Thank you," I said, watching the passing wall for a moment. The rest of the trip was, for the most part, quiet. Save for myself occasionally checking the remaining distance and informing Jonah of it, neither of us had anything more to say. Finally, when I could feel the air lightening around me, I swallowed the fresh oxygen and blinked.

"About one more minute," I said in an undertone. I wasn't entirely sure why I was whispering; we were still close to a mile below the surface. I blinked, returning my vision to normal, nodded at Jonah, and drew my sword as quietly as possible.

After a rather long sixty seconds, our ledge became level with the surface of the rest of the world, and the two of us stepped off. I lowered and rubbed my cramped hand, and the missing blood returned to it.

To my left, Jonah was chuckling to himself. "We should have thought of that the first time," he said. "Yes, it was about the same time of traveling, but it was a lot safer."

"You're forgetting I'm the only Draes in the Hishe army," I told him. "I'd have to ferry everyone back and forth for days."

"Right," he said. Then he addressed the sandy area that was completely void of people. "Hello!"

Nothing.

"We have your arrow."

At that, I looked down at Jonah's left hand, which was in fact clenched around the arrow, "I didn't even see you take that," I told him, and he grinned. As we stared around the empty space, a sudden thought occurred to me. "Maybe they left. It did take us an hour to get up here."

Jonah frowned. "I don't think so." He shook his head. "I think whoever it was wanted our attention for some reason."

"Well, they've got it," I said, slightly irritated. "Where are they?"

Suddenly, as if in answer to my question, a tall, cloaked figure appeared almost from nowhere. His face was completely hidden in the shadow of his hood, and he wore a long bow over one arm, a full quiver of arrows, and an empty, almost too-small blade sheath over his back.

"Is this yours?" Jonah asked, holding out the arrow.

The man nodded deeply, but when he spoke I could tell he was young. Young and almost British; he must have been some kind of far descendent from Raymond. "Yes. Could I have it back?"

I made to throw it back, but Jonah caught my arm. "That's dependent on your reason for shooting it at us in the first place," he said.

"I knew you would have a much easier time coming up than I would going down," the cloaked man said. "Plus, I didn't want to come down there and create a panic."

"Why did you need us?"

"I am an ambassador for my planet," he began slowly. "I'm sure yours has them, am I correct?"

I nodded; O' Maari was one.

"My king wants me to make contact with your four city rulers. I have since seen the first three, but in the city of Hishe, the king failed to tell me how to find Raymond Green." He paused. "Might you two help me?"

I was slightly dumbfounded and slightly relieved. He wanted *directions*? He had shot arrows into our camp and forced up the generals for directions! I wasn't sure what I had expected to find up here—in fact, I hadn't even thought about it on the way up—but I hadn't expected this. Next to me, Jonah frowned again and crossed his arms over his chest.

"Sandstiss," he said finally.

"The Hishe king told me that much," the man said. "I meant where …"

"South." I cut him off, pointing to the other side of Silver.

Though I couldn't see his face, I could only imagine the questioning look that now sat there. "Sorry?"

"If you walk about five or ten miles west of here, you'll see a bridge. Across it, it becomes a straight shot to that city," Jonah pointed out.

"Thank you."

"Are you lost?" Jonah asked, his voice slightly mocking.

"Kind of." The ambassador chuckled and shook his head. The sudden movement allowed his hood to slide back several inches so that it just fell the rest of the way. I knew now why he'd been wearing a hood. Underneath, his skin was so pale white that he almost flinched in the dimming sunlight. His jet-black hair was long and unkempt, and a long, thin scar stretched from right of his hairline over his eye and past his cheek bone. Jonah and I both sucked in a short breath, and the man laughed.

"What?" he demanded. "Never seen the effects of war, war boys?"

"Are you a soldier?" I asked. I had seen Shintie's scars—but none of them was on his face.

The man laughed again, giving off the impression that he was either insane or very good-humored. "Not all wars are fought on a battlefield, Zye."

I was taken aback, and so was Jonah. "How do you know my name?" I asked.

"Tag," he said simply, poking himself in the chest with his thumb.

I looked down to see that my dog tag had fallen from under my shirt and was sitting over the metal in plain view. I grabbed it and stuffed it, with some difficulty, back out of sight. The man gave a half smile of amusement.

"Thank you," he said. "I apologize for disturbing you."

He nodded in farewell to us, pulled up his hood, and vanished. All right, maybe "vanished" isn't the best descriptor, but it's close. He started running forward, toward Silver, but when he was ten feet away from the edge, he reached back as if to pull something from his empty sheath. He put his hand back down and flew off over Silver, standing on some kind of bright light.

"What do you suppose that was?" I asked after a moment of silence. "A riding star?"

"No way," Jonah said. His eyes were still fixed on the spot where the man had vanished. "If he was dumb enough to take off on a star that close, the force would have driven us halfway back to Hishe. No, I don't think it was a riding star."

"Well, I'm more than sure that even Draes can't fly." I frowned. "Come on; let's go back before it gets any darker."

8

CHAPTER EIGHT

Up until now, you've probably been questioning Hishe's method of training soldiers. Honestly, when Shintie first explained it to me, I thought it was ridiculous—until I realized that I had learned how to ride a horse and fight with a sword in the same way. Shintie had come up with a good analogy about X48's many training methods that made them sound much more sane. If there is something of dire importance at the bottom of an icy lake, the time it takes you to get to it doesn't change the temperature of the water. As the battles and fighting began in Silver, being thrown into everything at once seemed more and more logical—for the first three months, anyway.

It was near the beginning of our third month in Silver when the first battle between Scarlets and Ambers ended. It ended mainly when one of my swordsmen accidently killed a Scarlet. Yes, this game in the canyon was called war, but for the most part soldiers didn't die. We'd been ordered not to kill each other; that was one of two laws in the training ground. The other was broken later. The lanky swordsman who had killed the soldier was now refusing to even look at his bloody sword. He tried to leave the next night as well. Since the first night in the canyon I had become a light sleeper, and the heavy hoofbeats of his part-Shire woke me at once. I sprang lightly to my feet, pulled on a shirt, and pushed back the cloth flap of my tent. I saw him about twenty feet away, trotting carefully around the other tents for fear of running one over. Draft horses were never fast, and I caught him by the reins without even breaking into a run. I jogged along the trotting horse for several minutes until we were safely out of earshot of the rest of camp.

"Get off," I said, pulling back on the reins and showing him my face with a torch I had grabbed.

The boy slid from the high saddle and landed easily, knees bent. In the dim light of the flickering flames, I could tell he was shaking, nervous, and exhausted. There was no way he had slept last night.

"Just let me leave," said the teenager, trying to yank back his horse from me. "I'm not going to be a soldier if all I can do is kill the men on my side."

"Don't say that," I said, shaking his reins roughly. "Don't feel pity for yourself!"

"My apologies, Zye," he said with thick sarcasm. "What do you want me to do, continue as if I didn't just kill a soldier from my city?"

"It wasn't meant, was it?" I asked, keeping a safe hand on the huge draft's reins. "You were defending yourself and your army against an opposing army. People die in war; that's what being a soldier means."

"Then I have no desire to be a soldier," he said definitively, trying to heave the horse back up but causing no reaction.

"Do you honestly believe anyone here enjoys killing?" I asked, shocked by his answer, "Do you think someone here wants to be a soldier?"

He stood silently, not moving or speaking.

"All right," I said, getting angry and taking another tactic, "answer me this question. Suppose I actually allow you to leave the training grounds. Where on X48 are you planning on going, and what will you do once you're there?"

"I'll figure it out," he said.

I paused, wondering how long he had practiced this argument. "You can't go back to Hishe; you'd be executed. And you can't go to another city; no one would accept a runaway soldier. You don't have another place to go. Please see this reason."

"I understand what you're saying," he said, shaking his blond hair, "but I'm not going to fight anymore."

"Fine!" I gave up; I was exhausted and exasperated. "Fine, leave and get yourself killed. Just don't come back to haunt me because I was right." I threw the reins back at the soldier and dropped the torch, extinguishing the tiny circle of light. I stomped angrily back to my tent, not bothering to try and quiet the splashing of sand as I walked. Back on my cot, I lay facedown without removing my boots or shirt. I was too tired to stay awake and think but too angry to allow my mind to drift off. As a result, I stayed completely motionless for the rest of the night, almost falling asleep until some sound of the night brought back all of my senses.

The next morning, when Jonah and I were walking around the camp, I saw the boy I had told to leave last night. He met my gaze for a moment but looked away almost as quickly. I nodded to him without a word, somewhat calmed by the fact that he had decided to stay.

That day, one of the generals from the Scarlets rode into our camp. He suggested a week of official peace between the two of us so that they could bury their dead soldier and send a letter to his family. They also thought it would be a good idea to make all the weapons slightly intangible during battles. That way, even if someone were hit by something and injured, they couldn't die. Jonah and I both agreed at once.

On the second day of the week of peace, Henner and I took a walk to the wooded area of our camp to hunt. His older brother was a hunter, and the sport had always interested me, so he was going to try and teach me. Two hours later, I had learned nothing save for the fact that I would make a horrible hunter. I walked with heavy footfalls and slipped loudly and frequently. Whenever we actually saw something to hunt, I would turn to ask Henner something, and our prey would hear me and run off. Finally, he gave up on even trying, and the hunt became more of a leisurely stroll through the woods. I could tell that Henner went hunting with his brother a lot; he was almost invisible without even trying. Whenever there was a fallen tree or overgrown path, he could slip through or around it without leaving a trace of his existence. Given the silence of my companion, I didn't even notice when the birds had stopped calling.

"My brother always said birds are a good hunting tool," said Henner in a strange undertone. "When they stop singing, it means you're not the hunter anymore."

"What do you mean?" I asked, looking backward but seeing nothing.

"I mean," he said, raising his spear, "I think there's some kind of predator in this wood. It's too small for a cat, but I could see a wolf or a bear."

"You honestly think there's a wolf following us?"

"You never know what lives in an uncharted forest," he said, giving me some kind of creepy, sideways grin.

Suddenly, however, wolves were the least of our problems. In the dim light, I saw a flash of silver and heard a sword being drawn from a side sheath. Someone ran toward us and, before I had time to even think about my own blade, drove the sword right into Henner's chest. The person pulled back the now-scarlet metal and turned to face me. He was from Hishe, that I could tell, but he wasn't a soldier. He wore some kind of handsome, expensive uniform, and his sheath and sword hilt were both gold. I forced my hand around my own hilt and ripped out the blade it was attached to. In less than a second, the man spun around me faster than I could register with helpful panic slowing me down. As I made to face him again, I felt a pain in my back similar to that when I had cut my hand on a knife years ago. Only this pain was that multiplied by a hundred thousand. Without a single word, the man disappeared into the woods before I could even figure out which way he had started. I made to run after him but slipped in blood and fell to my back, paralyzed with pain. My vision flashed before my eyes, and I felt as if I were going to black out.

Sudden anger and fear threatened to overwhelm me, and I made no attempt to control them. I wanted to freeze time and teleport again; I wanted to kill this royal official and have him not even know what had happened. I wanted the power that came with being a Draes, not the weakness that came with being a human. However, Henner was a human, and nothing I did would ever change that. He was breathing hard, leaning heavily against a tree trunk, and gray faced.

"Henner," I said, for his sake ignoring the almost unbearable pain in my back, "can you walk or move at all?"

He said nothing, just shook his head. His teeth were clamped together and his eyelids half shut. He looked bad. His chest and shirt were blood soaked and his face twisted in pain. Even my ducking under one of his arms to take all his weight on myself made him give a soft groan. He was talented, though, and acted like a soldier. He made his best attempt to walk and act like the wound was nothing more than a scrape.

"If we can get back to the camp," he said after a moment of quiet limping, "I've got a healing knife in my bag; my older sister's a healer. It's under my cot, the middle one, in the tent left of yours."

"That's where we're going," I promised, making a mental note not to look at his bloody white face. Rye had tried to explain healing knives to me before. He said they were short hand blades with remedies and medicines inside. When a healer ran through the wound or heart with the knife, whatever was in the blade was injected into the person. Henner's sister was smart to give him a healing knife for training; whatever was in it would probably help a bad wound heal faster.

"Who do you think that was?" he asked, slipping in the packed sand.

"No idea." I shrugged. I moved my hand back to feel the gash I had received. There was almost nothing. I could feel my shirt, wet with sticky blood and torn by the sword. As my fingers found the slice through my skin, I could feel fresh blood, but that was it. There was a thin line where the blade had cut, but the wound was much smaller than it should have been. The man's sword was at least two inches wide, but by now, the gash in my back was centimeters long. *Draes must heal fast,* I thought. *I'll bet that's what helps keep us alive for so long.*

The walk back through the woods to the camp was slow and agonizing. Every step drained more color and blood from Henner while healing me and returning the little strength I had lost. Several times I had no other choice but to stop and allow Henner to rest, thinking to myself that we'd never find real daylight. We did, though. After three hours of trekking over the uneven ground, we stepped out into the rest of the canyon. Less than two miles away, I could see our camp, but two miles was another endless journey with a sword wound through the chest.

Angry at the lack of help and the dying boy on my shoulder, I lifted my head and shouted forward, "*Oy, somebody?*"

The words were magnified somehow, though I hadn't even tried to, and someone had heard. Less than half a minute later, I could make out two horses cantering toward us. As they drew nearer, I recognized Jonah and the boy who had killed one of the Scarlets. I was filled with relief.

"There's someone in the woods!" I shouted when they were close enough to be in earshot. "He's not a soldier or one of the trainers. I don't know who it is."

"He attacked Henner?" asked the soldier obviously.

I nodded frantically. "This is getting out of control; I've never heard of someone else being in this canyon, let alone some armed Hishe official."

"They were from Hishe?" It was Jonah. He had jumped off Fire Rain's back to take Henner's weight from me.

"I believe so; he had the uniform to fit." I paused and then remembered why I had called them over to begin with, "Henner said he's got a healing knife in his bag, but I doubt he could stay on a horse right now."

"Then you go on Fire Rain to get his knife, and you"—Jonah paused in his rapid speech to look up at the boy—"go warn the Scarlets about this man. I'll stay with Henner."

"I don't think I should go riding into Scarlet territory," he began.

Jonah cut him off impatiently. "Then send somebody else. Go on!"

He turned on his light chestnut and cantered back toward the camp.

Jonah handed me Fire Rain's reins, and I pulled myself up. He was taller than Starra, so it took a little more effort to get into the slim saddle.

"Ride fast, Zye." Jonah nodded to me. "We're on our way back behind you."

"I'll be back in five minutes," I promised Henner, and I dug my heels into Fire Rain's sides. He took off at once, not as fast as Starra but much, much smoother. I easily covered the two miles in about four minutes and found Henner's tent in something of a panicked calm.

I half dismounted, half leapt from Fire Rain's back and dove into the little shelter. Inside, there were three short cots with leather bags like mine underneath. I fell to my knees at the second and pulled it out. There wasn't much in the way of contents: half a loaf of bread, extra spear heads, the healing knife in a red case, and a dog tag. It wasn't Henner's, I knew. The back, which had been facing up, said the person's job had been a hunter. *I wonder if this is his brother's*, I thought, distracted. *Henner never told me his brother had died.*

He probably was dead, though—or close to it, if he was in the same condition as his tag. It was black with burned metal, and the gold ring outlining it, which appeared when someone got married, was scratched off in places. I couldn't read the name on the front because there was a good chunk of the tag missing. It was as if something with claws had raked through it, leaving it almost in two pieces. I tried not to imagine what it would be like to get killed by a wild animal until I remembered suddenly—*Henner!* I jolted with shock at forgetting him and lunched myself to my feet. Back outside, Fire Rain was a few yards off, grazing unconcernedly. With the knife case locked in my teeth, I jammed one foot in an iron and pulled myself on. When I had approached Fire Rain unannounced, he had spooked a little and almost took off with my left foot hooked in the stirrup. But he cantered off at my cue. I managed to stay on and righted myself as we went.

Jonah and Henner hadn't made it more than forty feet in the ten minutes it took me to get to the camp and reach them again. The only change in the two was that Henner was worse. I wasn't sure if he was conscious or not, but he wasn't bleeding anymore, and Jonah seemed to me to be more dragging him than helping him limp. Jonah himself was dark-faced and sweaty, and his teeth were clenched. When he saw me riding up on his horse, he lowered Henner to the sandy ground.

"He's about a minute away from dying, Zye," he said. "There's no use in that knife anymore."

"He's breathing," I pointed out, landing a little numbly from the tall horse.

"Hardly," Jonah said. "Soldiers are born to die, remember."

"Not before they're even trained," I said desperately. "We have to find that man."

"Zye." It was Henner. With an enormous effort, he had forced his eyes open halfway and formed the words, "Don't kill him; I don't want to take someone's head off for me. "

I opened his case and let the knife slide out into my hand. It was a beautiful knife, made for helping rather than hurting. I looked back at Henner in time to see him just manage to shake his head once. No. The movement made me angry that he was going to give up, but he seemed to realize this.

"Save that for someone you can actually save," he said, the last word curving up one end of his mouth into something of a smile. But then the smile faded, and his eyes fell shut again. His muscles became relaxed, and his breathing slowed and slowed. I stayed there, perfectly balanced in an uncomfortable, crouched position, and watched the teenager die. When his bloody chest finally rose and fell for the final time, I accepted the fact that he was gone.

Soldiers are born to die. We are, really, but are sixteen-year-old soldiers? Yes. You're practically born with your dog tag, with a destined name and a destined occupation. If you were born a soldier, you were born to fight and kill and die before your time. Henner was the second teenager to die in this canyon, but he was also the second son in his family. My mind went to his sister, the healer, who probably thought that giving him a healing knife would protect him. If only it could be that simple.

I stayed there for a long time after Henner was gone. At some point, Jonah left on Fire Rain, but I don't remember when. It was only when I realized it was almost too dark to see the body that I gave my own signs of life. I blinked and rested my hand, with the knife still clutched in it, on my knee. Then, slowly, knowing my muscles would be tight and cramped, I stood up. Night had more than begun to fall, and I couldn't even begin to see the camp anymore. I considered just sleeping there or burying him now but decided against it. As carefully as I could, I lifted Henner under one arm and propped him up as he had been before. I knew the direction and distance back to the tents, so I had no worry of getting lost. My only worry was of the attacker, who had come out of nowhere the first time, coming back and seeing that I had survived his sword wound.

As I walked, I wondered what had prompted the attack. The man had said not one word and probably thought that both Henner and I were dead right about now. In the morning, he would probably search the woods for the bodies and realize he hadn't been successful. *Maybe he wanted to see if we were Draes*, I thought, *or if I was. Why else would a man from Hishe kill his own soldiers knowingly?* The idea seemed more and more logical as I thought about it. I was right, that would make the attack an experiment, along with Henner's death. He wanted to know if a wound that would kill a human would kill me, which it didn't. This realization made me angry and frustrated, but not enough to lose my grip on things. I forced my head to stay on. On getting Henner's body back to camp … then the real war would begin.

9

CHAPTER NINE

I became a better general after Henner was dead. No one else, Scarlets or Ambers, died for the remainder of the year. Groups of armed soldiers would search for the man almost every other night but never found him. The slit in my back healed and scarred in less than a week, and the little blood I had lost was back before I fell asleep the next morning. Henner was buried not far from the stables, and soldiers would take shifts in exercising his horse but never riding it.

Not all of the soldiers believed that whoever had killed Henner had left me alone. That was the story I went with, that he had stabbed Henner and took off, but it was hard for even myself and Jonah (who knew, obviously, that it was a lie) to accept. I overheard, sometimes, soldiers wondering if I had been attacked and survived. Or maybe there was something just weird about me. Well, true and true, but I kept my mouth shut.

Whatever disbelief there was about me, though, died quickly. For the most part, the Ambers respected and trusted me, and they didn't want a reason not to. Slowly, even I started to forget Henner and the unknown man. That was, until the last week of training.

I was sleeping calmly, dreaming about O' Maari and how much the soldiers had improved in one year. I dreamed about returning home and seeing my family and about Carõ teaching me how to be a Draes and control my anger. Shintie told me that he sometimes dreamed about killing soldiers and them coming back to kill him, but so far I hadn't. Well, hadn't killed anyone yet, but at least my dreams seemed to leave Henner alone.

It was a probably an hour into the day when the hushed shouts of soldiers woke me up. At first, when I opened my eyes and only saw darkness, I was tempted to fall back asleep, but then I saw a dull flame ten feet away. It took me a moment to figure out the torch was hazy-looking because whoever was holding it was standing outside my tent, not in it. Half a second later, I was temporally blinded by the bright flame being brought into full view. I rubbed my eyes with one hand, propped myself into a sitting position with the other, and glared at the holder of light. Dark hair, tan-olive face, and an ever calm expression—it had to be none other than Maorin. He was standing beside another Amber, whose name, I believed, was Ocanal. In between them, locked in their tight grip, was a short, scraggly teenager. He was on his knees and looked as if he had been dragged halfway across the camp. Blood splotched his dirty clothes and skin, and his hands were tied behind his back, which seemed to be some feat. Over his back was a sword sheath like Jonah's, a full quiver of arrows, and a long bow. How even the three items, much less his hands, could all fit in such a small space was beyond me. His eyes, unlike his captors', were bright, alert, and angry; there was no sign of fear in the watery blue pupils staring up at me.

"Sorry to wake you, Captain," said Ocanal, "but we heard someone sneaking around the barns, and we found him."

"Is this the man who killed Henner?" asked Maorin indifferently.

"No." I said. "He was an official from Hishe, and he was older. This kid just looks like he ran away from home."

It had been almost a year since Henner's death, but I would never until I died forget that man's face. If I ever met him, I wouldn't kill him, though. I would always hate him for being the coward he was, but because of Henner's dying request I wouldn't kill him. Henner had never said I couldn't put him within an inch of his life, though. With failing curiosity, I studied this man—no, this teenager's—face. He was probably seventeen or eighteen, with dark brown-black hair that fell in limp coils around his face. His eyes were blackish, and his skin was the same tan-olive color as Maorin's, only darker.

"Who are you?" I asked, wondering if he would even respond.

He took a long time doing it but finally answered my question. "Austin."

"Are you a soldier?" I continued, even though I knew he wasn't.

He shook his head simply. He was calm and polite, just a little ticked off.

"Will you tell me who you are?" I asked, leaning the weight of my arms on my legs and staring right at the man.

His expression suddenly lighted immensely at my seriousness, and he even grinned. "You think I'm a spy or a Scarlet, don't you?" He laughed. "No, I just want to talk to you."

I was caught off guard a little, reminded suddenly of the man at the top of Silver who had shot arrows at us for directions. My humor was better now than it had been then, mainly because I hadn't had to travel an hour to point to a city this time. Maorin looked at me questioningly, and I nodded. "Sure. Maorin and Ocanal, you two can go back to sleep."

Ocanal nodded and backed out, but Maorin looked slightly concerned. "You sure it's not him, Captain?"

I shook my head. "No. I would know, believe me."

I could tell he was still unconvinced, but he left anyway, leaving Austin and me alone. With the two soldiers gone, he was able to stand up, but with some difficulty because he still didn't have the use of his hands. I created a small flame of light in one hand and let it hang in the air as I stood up and pulled out my knife. "I can get your hands," I offered.

With some double-jointed ability, the man lifted his hands over his head and down to my level so that I could saw through the thick rope. Once he was free, he thanked me and rubbed his wrists to get the blood flowing again. Now that he was standing unbound, I figured I could begin a normal—or as normal as possible in a war camp—conversation. "You never answered my question from earlier," I said, "about who you are."

"I'm Austin," he began. "I'm one step under your trainers. Basically, I get to mess with the groups as much as I want in the last few weeks. You're lucky you weren't a Scarlet; I had them about crawling out of the canyon in a night."

"What did you do?" I asked, half-fearful, half-entertained.

"You know what legend creatures are?" he asked.

"No." I shook my head.

"They're these huge half-animal and half-human hybrids that apparently did exist hundreds of years before Raymond showed up," he explained, demonstrating size with his arms. "Anyway, there was one really dangerous one called a wolfer, and people in the West End of Hishe would sometimes pretend to be them to scare kids. For some reason, no one would go in the woods, so one night I made myself appear as a wolfer and burst out of the trees. They've got a little wooded area like you, but they're a lot closer to it, so at once about fifty people saw me. To shorten my story, I scared the hell out of everyone."

"So what exactly is your job?" I asked, still slightly confused as to what point that had in training.

Austin pulled out a dog tag, covering the name side with his thumb, and showed me the back: trainer. "They're broad sometimes," he said, shrugging.

I resigned myself to sitting again on my cot. "Are you going to dress up and terrify all my soldiers as well?"

He looked amused. "No, don't worry. I figured I'd just talk to you, as I kind of made a mess of the Scarlets. Actually, I watched your training the past few days, and you have some pretty good fighters."

"Thank you." I nodded. "Sorry about Maorin and Ocanal, by the way. They didn't know you were a trainer."

"Clearly," he said. "They thought I was someone, though?"

I didn't respond for a moment, unsure about being able to trust him, but then gave in. "Near the start of the year, another soldier and I were hunting, and some man runs out of the trees and stabs him. He died a few hours later, and ever since then all of us have been on edge looking for him."

"Did you get to see his face?" he asked, serious again.

I nodded, fingering my knife.

"And he wasn't anyone you recognized—not a soldier or a trainer?"

"He wasn't even a teenager," I said. "Well, he was young, but not soldier-training age, more like nineteen or twenty." I paused and then remembered. "Hold on."

I ducked under my cot to grab my bag. After rummaging through it for a moment, I found what I was looking for and held it out to Austin. He took the folded piece of parchment and studied the drawing on it. It was the only time I'd ever attempted the skill, mainly because I didn't want to forget the man's face.

"Do you know who this almost looks like?" Austin asked

I shook my head.

"The prince, Kyre," he said, a little shocked. "Rainwin's son. Are you sure this is his face?"

"I will never in my life forget it," I said solidly, "but I've never met Prince Kyre. I can't compare faces."

"This is odd." Austin cocked his head. "Only soldiers and trainers should be able to get down here. Either it was the prince, or you now have an extremely powerful enemy."

"Should I be fearful?" I asked, looking down at my drawing when Austin returned it."

"I wouldn't be," he said reassuringly. "Yet, anyway. Can I know your name, by the way?" he added.

"Yeah." I nodded. "Zye."

"Carõ's little brother?"

I nodded reluctantly and asked what had been bothering me for some reason. "Could you explain your name to me?"

He looked confused. "Austin?"

"I've never heard a name like it," I said quickly. "It sounds like one you'd hear on—not here, but ..."

"Earth?" He offered and laughed when I nodded. "That would be because Austin isn't my real name; it's actually Airakon."

In all honesty, I liked the name. "Why don't you use it?"

"I like the Earth names better," he said simply. "I lived there for a few years, you know. I almost didn't come back."

I had no interest whatsoever in that planet. "You sounded like you knew my brother?"

"I knew him," he said, his voice darkened a little. "I trained him too, actually, and Shintie."

I didn't have time to hide the look of shock on my face before Austin saw it. If he had trained Shintie, that would make him at the youngest almost fifty. I knew Kylen and Lakin were that age, but they at least looked it. This man, with his bright eyes and brown hair, looked to be in his twenties at the most.

"Don't worry," he said, still chuckling, "I'm not a Draes."

I realized it had to be a joke, as most people thought the Draes were all long dead. I didn't entirely care, though, why he was still young. There was another thought bothering me. "Would you tell me what you did when Carõ was a soldier?"

Austin's face fell so fast it was almost comical. "He hasn't told you about that, has he?"

I shook my head. "Why, was it bad?"

"I was acting as a spy," he said. "It was actually what I was going to do to you, but this did not go as planned. He caught me and didn't believe a word I said. He didn't really know what to do with me, so he decided to have me executed before all the other soldiers in training. He was about to do it; he was completely ignoring my telling him the truth. That's when Kylen showed up. Your brother became furious. He was definitely embarrassed, but so mad too; he turned around and just punched Kylen as hard as he could. Broke his nose. I've never seen so much blood; he's got an arm. He was about to get me too, but I was quick enough to duck. It took me and two other big soldiers to hold him off Kylen till he was partly sane again."

O' Maari and I had always joked that Carõ was insane, but it was only because he was so in love with fighting and war. This, however, was a new kind of insanity; I'd never heard of anyone, a famous war general especially, losing his head like that. I made a bad, desperate attempt to defend him. "Are you sure it was him?"

Austin nodded darkly. "Oh, yes, it was him. That day, his trust of people was obliterated. He's the head general because he doesn't trust a soul. I'm honestly surprised he never left; he must really care about his brothers."

It was finally my turn to laugh. "He cares about nothing but war and acting as if he were my father."

"Being bossed around is a lot better fate then what his real soldiers get," Austin pointed out.

That took me off guard. "What are you talking about?"

"Why do you think Hishe hardly ever loses a battle?" he asked, breathing a loud huff of air. "What do you think happens to the first soldier who retreats?"

10

CHAPTER TEN

I realized as the week ended and we began our long ride home that Austin had just destroyed my last shred of respect for Carõ. All these years, I had blindly believed the stories of how amazing a leader my brother was, but now it was as if they'd never existed. The only thing in my mind for almost ten days after meeting Austin was images of Carõ ready to kill a trainer and doing his best to kill another. When I saw my house for the first time in a year, I was actually dreading opening the door and facing the man who I knew would be inside.

Luckily, Carõ wasn't waiting for me in the kitchen, at least. There were four people who were, though. The instant I closed the door behind me, I was engulfed in the tight hug of my mother.

"Oh, I missed you so much," she said. "You look so old now, and you're taller too. I can't believe that's all of you, though—you and Rye are trained fully now. My youngest boy is almost of age. Wow, that makes me old!"

"Mother." I grinned, gently escaping her tight grasp. "I'm seventeen; I'm not eighty."

"Oh, that's right," she exclaimed, "you turned seventeen a few months ago. Happy birthday, Zyemen!"

"Please don't call me that," I begged; she knew I hated my full name and usually only used it when I did something especially horrible.

"Be quiet," she snapped without real seriousness. "Your father liked that name. Anyway, I have something of his for you. Stay here."

My mother trotted from the room, and I turned to the three others standing around, Rye, Tahll, and Shintie. I moved toward my twin and hugged him tightly. "I missed you, Brother," I said when we broke apart.

I gave Tahll a small embrace, knowing he wasn't extremely affectionate. Finally, I got my bones crushed in Shintie's bear hug.

"Welcome home, soldier," he said when he knew I could breathe again. "And happy birthday, Brother."

I laughed; I was put in a good mood by my family. "What, are those thoughts not connected anymore?"

"No, they aren't."

I whipped around to find Carõ leaning in the doorway from another room. He was frowning seriously with his thick arms crossed disapprovingly over his chest.

"Carõ." I crossed the room to him, but we didn't embrace; I honestly couldn't remember the last time I had hugged him. Instead, I offered my hand, and he shook it roughly.

For half a moment, he studied my face. I could tell he was reading the change in my expression and the distrust in my eyes. He knew I knew something. "What happened?" he asked. Carõ was never one to beat around the bush.

"Austin," I said flatly. "I met him, and he told me about you."

He wasn't able to hide an angry snarl, but he tried to cover it up with an amazingly calm tone. "That was a long time ago. I was young and foolish, and I wasn't a good general yet."

"It still happened, Carõ," I pointed out.

He let out a low sigh and was about to respond when our mother reentered the room carrying a small package. "Here you are." She looked quite excited, as opposed to depressed and withdrawn, which was how she behaved whenever the subject of her dead husband came up.

She handed me the tiny box, and I pulled its thin brown wrapping off and removed the lid. Inside was a flat jet-black ring with the Latin inscription "Meus Filius" engraved into the metal. I frowned.

"My son," I said coldly. I was actually impressed that I could understand the two words. "What the hell does that mean?"

"*Zye!*"

"Sorry," I said quickly. "Thanks, Mother."

I left, walking quickly from the kitchen to my own room. First, I discover my own brother is a traitor and a murderer; second, I get a ring from someone I haven't seen in fourteen years. I slammed and dead-bolted the door and threw the ring into the fire grate. It created a little puff of ash when it landed and buried itself out of sight. It seemed to be heavier than normal metal; it had sunk through the tiny flakes of burned wood as if they were nothing more than beads of water. I spun around and kicked my wall, hard, but managed nothing but a sharp pain in my foot. Growling under my breath, I fell back onto my bed and pressed my hands to my eyes so hard that I saw spots. I stayed there for some time, completely exhausted, but my mind was too strained to even consider sleep.

For several hours, I lay on my back on my cot with my hands behind my head. In the calming quiet of the night, my head began to clear slightly, and by midnight I was about to fall asleep. About to, though, is the key term.

Thump! My eyes snapped open, and I pushed myself into a sitting position. There was no one and nothing in sight, but the sound hadn't come from my room. As quietly as possible, I pulled on a shirt and boots and crept into the hall. The thud had come from Shintie's room, and when I pushed back his door I found it vacant and the window open. For some reason, I felt a stab of panic, and I ran forward and dove headfirst from the second story.

All of us, even Tahll, had experience with jumping from windows, so it wasn't difficult to right myself and land on my feet. Once I felt solid ground under me, I bent down to feel for footprints in the sand. There was one, larger than mine, heading in the direction I knew to be the barn. At once, I took off, sprinting almost silently after my brother. I came to the door just in time to see Shintie taking off on his war horse, Armsted, in the opposite direction.

"Starra," I called, pushing myself into the dimly lit stable, "Come on!"

I heard several loud bangs from her stall, and she emerged a second later having kicked open the door. Because I had no idea where Shintie was going, I decided to throw on a saddle and bridle. In about a minute, I was tacked and mounted and racing off after my brother. After a few minutes, I found Armsted in the darkness and kept pace with him about fifty feet back.

It didn't take long for Shintie to realize someone was behind him, however. Without warning, he suddenly ripped out his sword, wheeled Armsted around, and managed to catch me right across the chest with the side of the blade. It wasn't an injury meant to kill—as if it could anyway—but it was still a sword wound. I shouted violently and slipped sideways out of the saddle, hitting my head hard against the ground. I heard Starra sliding to a stop somewhere to my left and rolled out of the way, hoping she wouldn't run into Armsted.

I wrapped my arm around my upper torso, applying as much pressure as possible to stop the bleeding. A few feet away, I saw Shintie seething by the light of a street torch. I didn't often see him angry, because for such a powerful soldier he was very levelheaded. He half climbed, half leapt from Armsted's back and threw a rough hand in my face. Without a word, I wrapped my fingers around his, and he pulled me up as if I weighed nothing.

"Go home, Zye," he said. He looked incredibly upset, but not because he had just tried to kill his little brother. "Why are you following me?"

"Because you were sneaking out of the house in the middle of the night," I said. "Where are you even going?"

"Nowhere," he lied. Like me, he was a terrible liar, and he knew I didn't believe him. "It doesn't matter, Zye. Just go."

"Only if you follow me," I said, my voice sounded dangerous like his. "I'm not letting you do something stupid."

"I'm not doing anything stupid," he protested. "I promise."

"Then what are you doing?"

The fight vanished from my brother's face then. He looked utterly defeated, shame and guilt replacing powerful defensiveness.

"Tie?" I asked, and I heard the fear in my voice. The fear sounded like that of a little kid. "What are you doing?"

The hulking, deadly soldier suddenly stepped forward and embraced me hopelessly. He wrapped his thick arms around my back, and I did the same, using up the entirety of my strength. It was then that I noticed that his hands were shaking slightly, and I gripped his armored shirt more tightly. "Raymond challenged me," he said finally.

Horror and shock replaced any other emotions, and I shrank back, away from my brother. I knew it was the last thing he needed at the moment, but I couldn't help it. "You promised," I said, my voice breaking. "You promised me ten years ago you never would!"

"I wasn't given the option," he said, trying to place a hand on my shoulder and looking hurt when I shrank away. "Chosen soldiers don't have the option to decline a challenge. That's why I never went with Carõ to his war meetings, and that's why I don't lead many advances. Zye, I don't want to fight Raymond Green."

"Then don't," I protested, my voice becoming pleading. "Come back home, Brother, please."

Shintie's grip on his hilt was becoming slack, as if he were losing the strength to even hold his sword. "I didn't want to tell you," he said. "I wanted to leave and not worry anyone."

"Until you didn't return the next day, anyway," I pointed out, admitting out loud the fact that I didn't think he had a chance. Of course he didn't have a chance; a dragon wouldn't have a chance against Raymond Green, "Tie ..."

"I'm okay," he said. He hugged me again and returned to Armsted, taking two tries to climb on. "But please go home."

I shook my head. "You know I'm only going home if you follow," I told him, pulling myself back into Starra's saddle.

"You're going to have to ride in rhythm with Armsted so it doesn't sound like there are a lot of people out in the middle of the night," he said, spinning his horse around in preparation to take off. "Also, keep about twenty feet behind me, at least."

I nodded; both were easy enough. It was actually why it had taken my brother so long to hear me in the first place. Without another word, Shintie turned his war horse around and took off at a wild gallop. The nice thing about Armsted was that he was almost as fast as Starra. The two of us had raced to our uncle's sword store once, and I had beat him by seconds. Even the fastest other horses would have been at least several minutes behind us.

I wasn't sure where Shintie was heading. I knew we would be leaving the city, one reason I had paused to saddle Starra, but as to how and where I was clueless. The four main gates were out of the question; all were guarded heavily and used a lot of time and energy to even crack. Not even Shintie's presence could force the guards to open the gates. Besides those, however, I was fairly confident it wasn't possible to exit or enter the city. Yes, it was big, but still, a massive wall surrounded the entire perimeter. I was about to ask my brother how he planned on meeting Raymond when he took a sudden turn down a narrow side street. I had to dig my heels into Starra's sides to get her to slow down enough to clear the change in direction. After that, he continued to make random, unannounced twists and turns, as if attempting to lose a pursuer. We rode at top speed in this manner for several hours, the sun slowly making its way up the side of the wall. It was nearly noon by the time we finally came to a massive stretch of stone. Slightly breathless, Shintie pulled Armsted back to a walk, and I did the same beside him.

"How do we get out?" I asked, pushing the sweaty hair from my face.

Shintie dismounted without answering me and strolled over to a nearby tree. He tied Armsted's reins in the unusual, impossible knot that only he himself knew how to undo and motioned for me to hand over Starra. I did and, as I always did, watched his hands work with the leather. However, I still couldn't figure out how he'd done it.

For another moment, I leaned against Starra's side as Shintie bade farewell to his horse. He had a remarkably strong bond with Armsted; I knew they had as good as grown up together, like Starra and I. From the corner of my eye, I watched my brother place a shaky hand against the horse's cheek and press his face against his.

"Tie," I said when he patted the stallion for the final time and forced himself away, "ready?"

Shintie drew his sword quietly and stepped in front of the wall, which looked solid and impassable. With two quick movements, however, he traced a hole just large enough for a man to climb out of. After a second, the lines on the stone became real, and with some effort, Shintie pushed the section of wall out of the way.

When he turned back to look at me, he seemed halfway amused by my shocked expression. He almost grinned. "You didn't think Father left through the north gate, did you?" he asked.

Honestly, the thought had never crossed my mind, but I guess it was true. "Is that possible everywhere?" I managed after a moment.

"No." He shook his head. "Father showed me where the weak points in the wall are a long time ago, in case there was ever a need to escape."

He paused, glanced back at the dimly lit city with a certain air of finality, and climbed through the small hole. I followed, making it through with more ease than him, given that I was so much smaller. Outside, I saw Red not yet overhead and took in the almost barren landscape. Across the black stretch of sand, I saw nothing save for some random, lonely plants. I was considering asking where Raymond was when I saw him.

He had appeared as if from nowhere. His jet-black cloak ruffled in a nonexistent breeze. I could see his sword sheath swinging by his leg as he made his way toward us. It was black with splashes of silver scattered along it, almost as if melted metal had been spilt on it by accident.

"Ah, Shintie," he said, revealing thick arms from under his cloak and spreading them outward slightly. "I was wondering when you would be here."

Shintie said nothing; he simply unfastened his cloak and let it fall in a heap behind him.

"Are you not very talkative?" the king continued. "You were when we met before; you had plenty to tell me."

I heard a low growl rumble inside my brother's chest.

Raymond smiled slightly. "Very well," he said. He was about to draw his sword when he seemed to notice me for the first time. "Oh, who's this?"

"Zyemen," I said. I guess then I wasn't yet smart enough to fear Raymond as much as I should, so I didn't know my disrespect would make things worse. "I'm his brother, and you're a horrible man to do this."

Raymond's smile widened. "To do what, young man?" he asked. "To challenge a very skilled and accomplished soldier into order to end the wars between the cities?"

I halfway glanced at Shintie. "What? How is this going to end anything?"

"If I win," said my brother, "Sandstiss is ours to do with as Rainwin wants. If he wins, nothing stands in the way of him taking over Hishe."

I hadn't thought of that. Shintie really was the main force that drove back Raymond's armies. He and Carō had held the old king at bay for fifteen years now; if either one of them died, we were helpless.

"Let us begin, then," said Raymond, slightly impatient. "I have matters back in my own city that have more importance than you."

Shintie gave Raymond another deadly snarl and turned to face me. He looked rather broken for a moment, but with an enormous effort he managed to compose himself. "Zye," he said, placing both hands on my shoulders, "If I don't win, you have to see to it that Raymond does not conquer the city. You're a strong fighter and a good soldier; I only wish I could have had you ride into battle with me. I love you, Brother."

I couldn't say anything; all I could do without losing it was hug him again. I didn't want to let him go, to watch him walk away and maybe—probably—not come back. I held on to his thick armor shirt until he forced himself to let go. I didn't protest, just watched him head toward Raymond with stony features.

The two men faced off with about ten feet between them. Each drew his blade, made a quick, not very respectful salute, and waited. The period of time before one of them moved wasn't very long—a few seconds, maybe. After that, both swordsmen launched themselves at each other, going for blood. I have to admit, I was worried about Shintie even being able to fight. He had been so shaky and terrified for the past twelve hours, I didn't know if he would be able to. I guess that's why he's the chosen soldier, though. No matter what emotions are felt, they vanish in battle. Shintie always told me that rage is blinding, fear is paralyzing, and confidence is weakening. I saw now that that was true, and that emotions can be your greatest downfall.

For how talented I knew Shintie to be and had heard Raymond was, I expected the fight to take a lot longer than it did. For a while, I watched each of them make violent stabs and attacks that were almost always parried by the other. They seemed to be pretty evenly matched; they were of similar height, weight, and build, not that physical characteristics had much effect on a sword fight. It was a matter of skill, and Shintie was the best there was. However, it was not even five minutes before I heard a lingering shout of pain from my brother and saw him fall to one knee. I clamped a hand over my mouth to keep myself quiet; if I ran forward, ran away, or so much as spoke a word, Raymond would automatically win. I watched my brother's back, praying for him to stand up, to grab his sword lying a few feet away, or to do something. I wasn't entirely sure what Raymond had done or where he had hit him, but I knew it was a serious injury if it forced Shintie to the ground. No injury, not even a broken leg, had ever gotten the best of my oldest brother. He was the strongest man I had ever met.

Raymond twisted his arm around and drove it forward. Shintie was rocked backward with the force, and when the king drew back his hand the soldier fell to his back. In only a few minutes, Raymond Green had defeated the greatest soldier in all of Hishe.

11 CHAPTER ELEVEN

For about a second, I stood there too shocked to move. Then I wrenched a short dagger from my belt and pelted it at Raymond. The knife flew an inch away from his face; however, he vanished. He disappeared into thin air, and the dagger fell rather pathetically to the ground.

Shintie wasn't quite dead when I rushed over to him. His eyes were bright and open, and his breathing was calm and steady. If it weren't for the two gaping holes in his chest, I could have believed he was fine. He looked almost pleased with something.

"Tie," I said, dropping to my knees beside him. I didn't really have anything else to say besides that.

His mouth turned up in something of a smile, and he struggled with his draining strength to reach for the chain around his neck. When you were dying was about the only time the dog tag chain was weak enough to break, but even so it took him a great deal of effort to do so. Holding his tag by the two ends of the broken string, Shintie pushed it into my hand. I wrapped my trembling fingers around his for a moment and sat there until the rest of his life faded away. When he was gone, my strength failed me. I fell forward and laid my head against his chest, sobbing and pleading for him to wake. In the endlessness that I stayed there, he never once answered me.

The thing that got me up was the horses. I had almost forgotten them, tied to a tree probably not more than fifty feet away. I forced myself to my feet, shrugged Shintie's body over my shoulders, and crawled back through to the city.

Starra and Armsted stood tied expectantly to their tree, waiting for us. Upon seeing Shintie, the old stallion dropped his head with an almost human expression of grief. I couldn't bear to look at him; he looked too much like his owner. Instead, I took out my sword, cut the two of them loose, and pulled myself with some difficulty onto Starra's back. My brother still hooked over one arm, I tied Armsted's reins to a bag ring on my saddle and started back home at a walk.

It took several days to cover the distance Shintie and I had traveled in one night, but all throughout I never lost any energy. I was never hungry or thirsty, and whenever I saw other people I would slide down a side street. I wasn't ready to face people just yet. The only time I ever stopped was to allow Starra to rest or drink water. Armsted always refused; he, like me, was still too sick to even consider it.

12
CHAPTER TWELVE

On X48, it's customary that, when necessary, fathers single-handedly bury their sons. However, when that wasn't possible, the task fell to the oldest son. Carō was in a war meeting and unable to be interrupted until late. Going in order of age, the second-oldest son would be Tahll, but the idea of Tahll doing manual labor, even if it was burying his brother, was still laughable. As a fully trained healer, Rye was needed in a healing ward until late, like Carō. So, naturally, the task fell upon me, the youngest son and brother.

After sitting in a saddle for five days straight, I could not force myself to ride even Starra or Armsted. Instead, I balanced Shintie's body over my shoulders, fitted a shovel in a makeshift sheath on my back, and walked the nearly thirty-mile trip to the soldier graveyard on foot. I left my house before the sun starting rising, but by the time my eyes caught sight of the first headstone, Red was sitting directly overhead, burning the back of my neck. The guard outside the chained gates was asleep in a chair, his chest moving up and down in a slow, calm rhythm. He wore handsome armor, not for a soldier, really, just more for show, and his blond hair was tied back with a strip of leather.

I didn't have the patience or energy to wait for him to wake. "Sir!" I said loudly. "Sir, please open your eyes."

The guard jolted awake and took a moment to fix his coppery eyes on me. "Hello there," he said, not looking at me but on the dead man on my shoulders. "Who are you?"

"I am his brother," I said, indicating Shintie, "and he is the chosen warrior of Hishe."

"Shintie," breathed the guard, and I could see the grief in his face. "What happened?"

"He tried to take on Raymond Green on his own," I said a little hopelessly. "He failed."

The guard fumbled with a key ring on his belt, hiding his shocked face from me. I knew he was trying not to look upset. Everyone was going to be heartbroken when the word of my brother's death became common knowledge. For the moment, however, I and my brothers and mother were the only ones with the right to mourn him.

I followed the guard through the grave area, passing row upon row of endless headstones. I guess I hadn't realized until now just how many soldiers had died for Hishe—hundreds of thousands, probably. We walked for at least a mile, neither of us speaking, until we came across an unfinished row.

"Here," he said, gesturing to a plot of land without a grave behind it. "Is anyone else coming later?"

"My brothers and mother will be here an hour or so before dusk. Until then, however, I will be alone," I said, setting Shintie's body on the black sand and pulling out the shovel from the sheath on my back.

"Let me know if I'm needed," offered the guard, turning to leave. "I am very sorry about your brother."

"Thank you."

The blond-headed guard bade me good-bye, and I stood before my brother's not-yet-existing grave, listening to the sound of the guard's retreating footsteps. Unable to help myself, I glanced at the last grave before Shintie's and was taken aback by the name: Henner. I crouched down before it for a better view, but my eyes had not been mistaken; it said "Henner. Age: seventeen years. Weapon: spear. Death: training." I felt a pang in my chest until I reminded myself I wasn't here to feel sorry for myself. I leaned on my shovel staff to push myself to my feet, returned to Shintie's plot, and began to dig.

For a couple of hours, I dug without pausing, not to rest, not to eat or drink anything, and not even to escape the heat of the blistering sun for a moment. At some point, I unclasped my scarlet cloak and covered Shintie's body with it, afraid of the heat's effects on him. Under my cloak I wore brown leather leggings and a cloth shirt, which provided little protection from Red. By the time I had dug through two feet of sand and found some sort of clayish soil, I could feel my entire back burning.

The wet soil wasn't a thick layer in the planet; it was more like a barrier between the sand and what was underneath. After removing less than a foot of the stuff, I went to return my shovel to the ground and was stopped abruptly by something very determinately solid. I cursed to myself, having been hoping the next layer would be farther down. I knelt down to remove the rest of the soil by hand, feeling the ironlike clay brush under the tips of my fingers.

If you've been wondering about a coffin for my brother, people on X48 aren't buried in wooden boxes. The tough clay that makes up most of the planet's inside is molded around the body to make a coffin much more durable than a cut-up tree. I could still remember watching Carõ and Shintie molding out a huge grave for my grandfather's horse. The task took almost a week to complete. Luckily for me, Shintie's size did not match that of a Belgian, and I was able to shape the clay to the appropriate dimensions within four hours.

I stood up, my back muscles sore from being hunched over for so long, and pushed myself out of the grave with two hands. For a long time, I stood over the hole, slightly transfixed and unable to move. I didn't want to force myself to do what I had to next: covering up my oldest, favorite brother and never seeing him again. I crouched down beside him, pulled him halfway on to one shoulder, and half carried, half dragged him to the hole. Exhausted from the day, it was all I could do but lower him in from above. I no longer contained the energy to climb into and out of a grave again. Once he lay on the hard clay on his back, his eyes shut and his wounds covered, I could almost kid myself that he was only sleeping—or even unconscious.

For a moment, nothing happened. Then, very slowly, the clay began to move on its own accord. It slid out from all sides, a few inches over Shintie's face, making its way toward the middle of the rectangle. It took about a minute for the clay to completely hide my brother. Once it did, it crackled lightly like drying flames and turned a polished black color. I knew now that there was not a force in existence that could ever uncover my brother again.

I didn't like looking at the hardened clay where my brother used to be, so as quickly as possible I returned the grainy soil to its original place. The jet-black sand filtered in on its own—not by magic, just gravity. I smoothed the uneven sand with the back of the shovel until the grave plot looked as it had before. *I would never guess so many people are buried here,* I thought, sheathing the shovel and pinning my cloak back on. *The planet hides people so well.*

By glancing at the sun, I guessed that my family wouldn't be here for another few hours, but I didn't have the energy to do anything else. I bent down on one knee and leaned some of my weight on the blade of the shovel, now resting in the sand. I was halfway sleeping when the sound of boots splashing through the sand snapped me awake. I didn't turn to see who it was, and I didn't say anything to acknowledge them; I only knelt there and prayed it wasn't Carõ.

"Zye?"

I let out a breath of relief and turned to face my twin. He was standing with his weight on his left leg and his cloak pulled a little too far to the right; he was trying to hide the fact that he was injured, "Are you all right, Brother?" I asked, straightening my knees to again find my feet.

"I fell off Mason," he said slowly, "and I'll live through that, if that's what your question was. If you mean about our brother, I suppose I'll have to say that death happens. After all, two of my brothers are soldiers."

"Are Carõ and Tahll coming?" I asked, not bothering to ask about our mother; I knew she would come.

"Tahll's on his way," Rye said, "Carõ's still at Rainwin's manor, but that's not very far away."

When I was young, I used to pretend I was Hishe's chosen soldier. I would sprint through the horse pastures murdering hundreds of enemies in single blows. Nothing could stop me; when a soldier did hit me, I would fall for a moment but then jump back to my feet and take down whoever had "killed" me with a new vengeance. Now, that game just seemed idiotic. There was no difference between a common soldier and a chosen soldier except skill. The only known man to survive a fatal attack is a Draes, and in most books they aren't men, so that doesn't even count.

13
CHAPTER THIRTEEN

Somehow, I managed not to break down after my mother, Carõ, and Tahll arrived. My mother didn't even try (as well she shouldn't have) to hide her tears, and Rye and Tahll were gone soon after her. I'm not sure if it's just the war and death mentality of life or what, but neither Carõ nor I even blinked. The five of us stood around the grave plot until there was no light left and even I couldn't see the ground anymore. Carõ, Tahll, and my mother returned home, and Rye returned to the healing ward. I still didn't have the energy to move, and I was too tired to sleep, so I stayed there all night, crouched down on one knee. Alone in the darkness, my mind struggled over two ideas: one, of course, to avenge my brother's death, and two, to fight as the soldier I knew he would want me to be. I knew I couldn't do both, because if I took on Raymond, he would probably find some way to kill me, and if I somehow killed him, I would be out of a job. On the other hand, I could continue to defend Hishe, like he had for some many years, but keep in mind the fact that the man who murdered him was still out there. By the time the sun was fully risen again, I hadn't come to a decision. Luckily, I was temporarily distracted.

"Zyemen!"

Even after going through the night with no sleep, I still didn't jump when a rough voice broke my perfect silence. I didn't turn to see who it was, though; it wasn't one of my brothers, so I didn't care. I just kept my tight position and my mouth shut.

"Zyemen, get up," the voice repeated. "You're needed somewhere else."

For a long time, I didn't move or speak, and neither did my visitor. After almost five minutes, however, he became impatient. I heard the slicing of metal over metal as a sword was drawn and I chuckled out loud (the first sound I had made in about twelve hours) when I felt the cool blade resting on my shoulder.

"Not a good idea," I said slowly, still not moving.

"I'm not going to pretend I know how to kill you," said the unknown man, "but if I have to cut you into hundred pieces to get you to my father, that's what I'll do."

"And who might your father be?" I asked with sarcastic interest.

"King Rainwin," said Prince Kyre.

I had never met the prince before, and so far I didn't like him. He had, as Carõ had told me for years, an air of false importance that no one and nothing could destroy. "Get lost," I said after a moment. "I'm not in the mood to argue with your father, and I refuse to argue with you."

The sword was withdrawn and sheathed in a quick, irritated motion. "Get. Up," he said pointedly. "You can walk with me, or I can pull you by your hair—your choice."

The mental image of Prince Kyre pulling a soldier back to his father's manor by the hair caused me to laugh again. Despite myself, however, I finally straightened my locked muscles and reached my feet. Rubbing my stiff arms, I turned to face Prince Kyre, seeing him for the first time in my life, and almost lost my ability to stand. I was staring into a face that I knew I would never forget, a face that had been forever imprinted into my memory.

"You" was about all I could manage. I felt as if the energy and fight had just been sucked out of my body. There was a dull sense of blind pain and angry guilt in the back of my mind, but the plain shock of who Prince Kyre really was, was too overwhelming.

"You recognize me?" he asked, his voice half-amused. "I wondered if you would. It was dark in those woods."

"Yours is a face I will never forget," I assured him, turning away from him. "And if I could ever have respect for a prince, I've lost all of it for you."

"I'm not looking for it, Zyemen," he said. "I just need to get you to my father."

I walked forward a few yards, past Henner's grave plot, so that if Kyre followed me, he would be forced to see it.

"I'm not going to apologize for what I did. I had reasoning behind …"

"*Behind what?*" I shouted suddenly, cutting him off. "Behind killing a soldier, not only a soldier who was more than willing to give up his life to protect you, your father, his city, and everyone in it but also a soldier who wasn't even seventeen, a soldier who hadn't even been in a battlefield yet.

You killed one of your own, Kyre. What reasoning did you have behind that?"

At that point, I left. I was too upset and furious and disgusted about learning the identity of Henner's murderer to wait for an answer. I walked off for about ten feet but quickly broke into an all-out sprint. I lowered my head and pounded away from the prince, away from the graveyard, and (I wished) away from everything. I wasn't sure how long I kept going, but it must have been for a while, because when I was again aware of my surroundings I was in a tree in Shade Under. Actually, I was in the tree by O' Maari's and my usual campsite, thirty feet in the air. I was slowly catching my breath, and there was dried blood on my hands. I didn't waste much time in wondering what I had done, though, because I decided I didn't care.

I was hunched down on a thick branch of the tree, my back resting against the uneven bark. From the feel of it, I could tell I had lost my shovel at some point. I was resting most of my weight on the balls of my feet; balanced in such a position that I knew even shifting my weight would mean falling. Carefully, I turned my cramped neck to look below; there he was. He was sitting against the tree I was perched in, his head resting back against the bark. I knew there was no way to get down without him noticing, and I would have to face Rainwin eventually anyway, so I let my weight shift to the side and fell to the ground. The wind whipping against my face, even for a brief moment, felt wonderful. I landed on one knee and one foot, my fingertips touching the sand to steady me. Beside me, Kyre glanced up from a book in his lap, completely unperturbed. He had probably been expecting me to fall out of the sky for several hours now.

I got shakily to my feet and waited for the prince to say something. He snapped the book shut with one hand, slid it inside a bag on his shoulder, and pushed himself to his feet. "Are you ready to cooperate?" he asked tiredly.

Several sarcastic comments ran through my mind, but I held them back, reminding myself who I was talking to. There was no good impression Kyre could make on me now, but he would be my king one day, so I had to at least pretend to respect him. "Yes," I said, "and allow me to apologize for my difficulty earlier."

"Apology accepted," he said. He still had that annoying air of overconfidence, but it was less than before. "We're a few hours' ride from my father's manor. There are two horses waiting at the entrance to the forest."

I really didn't want to ride a horse again, especially one that wasn't Starra, but I decided I had done my fair share of walking. The two of us made our way through the trees in silence, neither of us wanting to talk. The sun sat slightly more than overhead. I knew it was probably a few hours past noon. Several yards away from the first trees stood two tethered black horses. They were tall and beautiful creatures with expensive-looking tack that could probably be traded to feed a small family for a year.

"Follow me," said Kyre, patting the closer of the two horses on the neck, untying him, and pulling himself into the saddle. I did the same, struggling slightly with the bulky saddle because it was of western style, not English as I was accustomed to. We rode as we had walked, not speaking. I followed about twenty feet behind the prince, slightly to his left, as we cantered down the almost-empty roads. After a little more than an hour, I caught up with the prince and asked the question that had been bothering me.

"It's because of your brother," he said, nodding at a vacant market as we passed it. "It's everyone else's turn to mourn the loss of the chosen soldier of Hishe."

The thought of almost a million people crying over my brother sent a fresh wave of hatred through me. He was my brother; no one even knew him save for a few dozen. What right did anyone else have to be upset that he was gone? The city hadn't shut down eight years ago when an old general had died. What was the difference? None of this I asked, of course. I merely grunted to myself and let Kyre gain back his lead.

We arrived at the Hishe manor in a little less than four hours. Besides the one comment about Shintie, we never spoke a word. My resolve to ignore him, however, was broken when my eyes found the immense house. Carō had told me the building was large and impressive, but I had never believed his descriptions until now. Behind twenty-foot-tall, silver-and-gold gates and a wide courtyard sat a five-story mansion with vast double doors to match the gates and thick windows with glass panes (something that even my family couldn't get a hold of). Standing in the middle of the courtyard was a man who I could only guess was King Rainwin. He was tall and thin, not very muscular, and wore a silvery-gold cloak over majestic-looking armor. He had a long sword belted on his hip. It, like his son's, was solid gold.

Both of us dismounted at once and sank onto one knee. In all honesty, it surprised me that even Kyre had to bow to his father. I wasn't about to tell him that he was on the same level as a king, but I thought there would be more of a fatherly bond. Guess not. As Rainwin made his way toward us and I pushed myself back to my feet, I saw something trotting at his heels. At first I thought it was a wolf, as many people in Hishe kept them as pets. However, as it broke into a heavy gallop at Kyre I realized it was definitely not any wolf I'd ever seen. It was a fully grown caracal cat. Ten feet from the prince, it launched itself into the air, landed on his chest, and nearly knocked him over. He pivoted around on one foot to keep his balance and waited for the cat to let go.

"Hello, Taun," he said, scratching it under the chin. "It's nice to see you."

"Why does it not surprise me that you have a pet wild cat?" I asked, eyeing it cautiously.

The caracal rounded on me, flattening its black-tipped ears against its skull and showing off pointed fangs.

"You should speak for yourself about being wild, Draes."

If it hadn't been a female voice that spoke and I hadn't seen her mouth move, I would never have believed I was talking to a cat. I simply stood there, mouth gaping in disbelief, because I was sure Kyre's pet had just spoken plain English.

"What's the matter," she asked with annoyance, "have you never seen a caracal before?"

"Not one that could talk," I said, wondering if I was still asleep in the grave area. "How ..."

"Every living creature with a mouth has the ability to learn other languages," she explained. "Only English is difficult, so most nonhuman animals don't bother. Kyre taught me how to speak with people before I learned the language of my own kind."

"Are you saying any animal can speak?" I asked, all my past emotions completely wiped out. "Can horses?"

The caracal looked more offended than annoyed now. "You've heard a horse whinny and nicker, right? You've heard a wolf growl and bark? Tell me the difference between that and the language of humans."

"Tauna," said King Rainwin. I hadn't even realized he had crossed the courtyard and was standing before us. "Zyemen meant no disrespect to you. He will apologize kindly."

A little taken aback, I nodded and crouched down to the caracal's level. "I'm sorry, Tauna," I said honestly. "I truly did not mean to offend you; I was only surprised."

She seemed pleased by this and purred slightly, rubbing her small head against my knee. "I am easily offended and easily appeased," she said. "Kyre, let's go inside."

As Kyre and the lynxlike animal trailed away, Rainwin chuckled slightly, "My son told me he wanted a pet to teach it to speak when he was ten," he told me. "I was only humoring him, as I did not believe for a second he could make a cat talk. Nine years later, however, a prince made a king eat his words. Would you ever think a king could be wrong, Zyemen?"

"I honestly thought, though they are as human as most, that kings could not make mistakes," I admitted slowly.

Rainwin continued to laugh. "You and the rest of Hishe," he said, "and that is why bad things happen. My son proved to me that there are things I do not believe in and proved that I can be wrong. If I, the sole ruler of a quarter of this planet, can have faults, that means Raymond Green does as well."

Raymond Green was not where I was expecting him to go with the conversation, and the mention of the name sent a new wave of pain through my mind.

"Zyemen," he said, all composure regained, "I cannot tell you how sorry I am. I know you had an exceptional bond with Shintie. However, I didn't bring you here to show you pity. There is a pressing matter at hand; we have no chosen soldier."

Again, I was taken aback. "Why does that involve me?" I asked. "I'm seventeen. I'm not even old enough."

"You are Shintie's brother and closest friend. Everything he knew he taught to you. Am I wrong?"

I shook my head.

"The city's sole protector is not chosen because of skill or age or experience; he is chosen because of heart and willpower and strength. Many people have been watching you over the years, Zyemen. They are confident that you are the one we need, the one who will once and for all bring peace to X48."

"Do I get a choice?" I asked hopelessly.

"Everything is a choice, Zyemen," he said, "and only you can make those decisions. I am only advising you to help your city in a way that you will never be able to again."

Could I really say no to Rainwin? Was I allowed? I knew the answer to that. "I will, sir," I said, giving up.

"Good man." He smiled at me, placing a reassuring hand on my shoulder. "Don't let me regret this, Zyemen. There are thousands of others much more able than you who would be happy to take your place, but I have faith in you. Now, you can go home and rest; you'll need it. Carõ will tell you when you're needed again."

I made to leave, but one last question slipped out before I could. "Do you know what Kyre has done, sir?"

"He took the life of a Hishe soldier." Rainwin nodded. "I know; he told me the day after he did it. You have every right to be angry with him, but let me tell you, it was his pride in his city that led him to do that. He holds a lot of anger with Draes, and he thought you were one; he had to know for sure. I should have told him, but I never thought in a thousand years that he would openly attack two soldiers."

"His name was Henner," I said. I felt as if I were required to say this. It felt like the least I could do for him now.

"I know."

"Did Kyre tell you why he killed Henner along with me?" I asked.

Rainwin breathed heavily. "Honestly, he told me he didn't know which one you were. He was trying to find you. A soldier at your camp told him you were hunting, and he went to the woods. You and your friend were the first people he saw."

"Henner's death was an accident," I realized numbly.

"All are," the old king told me. "Now go home. You'll need your energy soon."

14 CHAPTER FOURTEEN

Rainwin offered me a horse to ride home, but I refused. It took the rest of the day and into the night to walk on foot back to my house. Even after several days of not eating, I still wasn't hungry, because there was still one more thing I had to accomplish. One thing, then my life could to back to how it was—sort of.

"*Carõ!*" I slammed his door shut behind me after entering his room.

When I had entered my dark house, I had found that no one was awake. So naturally it was a safe guess that my now oldest brother was. When I came in without warning, he looked up from a spread of maps on his desk but wasn't startled. Carõ doesn't startle. I was done with waiting on him, though; he was about to give me the answers I wanted.

"Zye, you should go to bed," Instantly, his voice became that of a father trying yet again to teach a very young child. "You've been awake for days now."

"Where is he?" I demanded, ignoring his probably correct suggestion.

"I beg your pardon?" He stood up just to make himself taller than me.

"*Where can I find Raymond Green?*" My fingers itched for my sword hilt, but I controlled myself. "Where can I find him and kill him?"

His expression changed at once. "You don't need to go kill the man who found and brought order to this planet," he said, still in the annoying parental tone.

"That man killed my brother," I pointed out, balling my fists, "and yours, if you're still mine."

Carõ pressed his lips together. "You both are my brothers," he said, "but killing someone won't bring someone else back."

"Sandstiss would crumple and die without him," I said, actually finding pleasure in the thought, "just like Hishe would without you. Don't you want that?"

"I do want Raymond gone," admitted Carõ, "but as a general you learn that there are right and wrong ways to do things. Raymond wants war; that's how he plans on taking over Hishe. As a general, I am going to honor that."

A small explosion went off in the back of my mind. "Carõ," I started, slightly shocked by his response, "are you not upset that Shintie's dead?"

"Of course I am, Zye," he said, "but he was a soldier. Soldiers die."

"Raymond's a soldier," I pointed out, "and he needs to die!"

"What makes you think you even have a chance against Raymond?" Carõ asked wearily.

"I'm Hishe's chosen soldier now." I shrugged. "That—"

Carõ cut me off by laughing so hard I was sure he would wake someone up. "Did you never listen to Shintie? All of that, 'Titles don't matter; I'm still a man. I will still die a normal soldier's death.' I thought he taught you all he knew?"

"He did!"

"Then listen to him," the general snapped. "He was smart. You are a soldier, Zyemen, not an assassin."

I left then, wheeling around and storming back to my room. I threw myself facedown on my cot and pressed the back of my head with my hands as if I were trying to push myself through the mattress. I stayed there for a few hours, listening to Rye's steady breathing. I knew he was awake, but I didn't have the energy to talk to him. It wasn't until I couldn't stand lying still anymore and made to return to Carõ's room that he finally spoke.

My hand was on the door when Rye's voice came up. "Don't follow Shintie, Brother," he said. "Raymond isn't worth two of us."

I ignored him and found Carõ still up, but now lounging on his cot reading a book. He glanced up when he heard my footsteps but didn't greet me.

"Just tell me where he is, Carõ!" I said. "Please. I have an advantage; he can't kill me."

"No," mused my brother, "only chop you up into a thousand pieces so that even Rye can't put you back together again." He paused for a moment, as if it pained him to say his next words. "I'll take you."

Great. Another chance for my older brother to show me up. Despite the fact that it sent a flood of relief through me, it wasn't what I wanted to hear. "I can take him myself."

"Zye, you can't take me yourself," he said, setting down his book and belting on his sword and sheath, "and I can't take Raymond."

"Then why—"

"We might be able to together," he cut me off.

"Fine."

I followed him down the stairs and out the front door, both of us walking in complete and total silence. Outside, it seemed colder than before, and the air tasted like rain. We trotted out into a field for several minutes, creating enough distance so that taking off on a riding star wouldn't cause so much damage. When Carõ was satisfied with the space, I conjured two stars, and we took off. As we shot away from Hishe, I glanced back to check for destruction. The blast of wind created when we left had blown over the tall grass and bent a nearby fence.

When we were shooting over the city and safe from anyone's hearing, I made an attempt at a conversation. "How far off is Sandstiss?" I asked.

Carõ shrugged. "At our speed now, less than an hour."

"How big is it?"

"Larger than Hishe."

"How many people have tried to kill Raymond?"

"*Zye!*" he said, getting aggravated. "Will you just fly?"

I shut up after that, and we flew in silence save for the wind whipping around the riding stars. Raymond's city ended up being almost an hour and a half away from Hishe. When I asked Carõ about the difference in time, he suggested that maybe the citizens had pushed the wall farther away. I didn't laugh, for at that point a solid black line, darker than the sand, appeared in the distance.

"There it is," called Carõ.

"Sandstiss," I breathed, my eyes fixed on the wall, which was slowly growing larger and larger.

"Are you sure you want to do this, Zye?" he asked. "Put reason to what you're planning. Raymond killed Shintie, and I had a hard time winning against him. You can't win against me. How were you planning on even going about this?"

"When I fenced against you and Shintie," I began with gritted teeth, "I was only fencing. Also, I didn't have a reason to actually kill you. I couldn't care less about the right way to avenge someone; I'm not only using a sword."

Carõ shut up; he knew what I meant. I might not be as good of a swordsman as Raymond, but I was an equal if not stronger magician. I was confident that between the fight being two on one and my abilities, we could at least hold our own. As we drew nearer and nearer, I pulled out my shoulder knife (a knife that most people kept in a small hold on their arms), gripped it in my teeth, and tugged hard with one hand.

"What on X48 are you doing?" Carõ asked, glancing sideways at me.

"Extending my knife." I did so and tucked it under one arm. "Two swords, just in case."

"Put that thing away, Zye. You can't handle two swords at once. Most top swordsmen can't handle two swords," he said without humor. "Focus."

I held out my real sword behind me and slid my shoulder knife into my sheath. The knife was only a saber in comparison to my broad sword, and it rattled violently in its too-big hold. I took a deep breath and watched the Sandstiss wall grow bigger and wider. In another few seconds, we passed the wide, stone brick wall and slowed enough to watch the beginning of the city pass underneath us. It wasn't very impressive.

People darted through the streets, afraid to be seen, and gray, dismal buildings barely stood with violent chunks blasted out of the sides. There were no trees or even barns or horses. Even on the outskirts of my city, I had never seen such a poor area, so I was even more surprised when Carõ began descending and slowing.

"What are you doing?" I asked in a low undertone. "Why not fly to the manor?"

"We're there," said my brother pointedly, and he gestured to a huge black building maybe a mile away.

"That's Raymond's home?" I asked in disbelief. "It's really this close to the wall?"

"Sandstiss is very different from Hishe," Carõ explained, "Remember, Raymond is from a country where its capital sat on the rim. He saw and lived in its poverty and wealth, so he does nothing to help those who aren't as well off as others."

I thought that was a strange reason not to help people, but then again, it was Raymond. Plus, even if you weren't rich, you had to try pretty hard to become poor on this planet.

"Also," Carõ continued as we landed and began walking through the dingy streets, "a lot of the money these people have is taken away by soldiers and guards; you should see the armies Raymond has. You know,

I'd bet that at least a third of the city's population gets made into soldiers, whether they're meant to or not. I'll bet you Raymond doesn't care; the only things he obsesses over are numbers, not skill."

"That doesn't seem very intelligent," I mused. "The people who aren't meant to be fighters can't make good ones."

"True." Carõ nodded. "But think about Raymond's reasoning; one army has a hundred good and talented soldiers while his has ten thousand men wearing armor and swords. Don't think everyone knows who I am because I won fair fights."

"Then haven't you proved that a hundred to one is a bad idea? Did Raymond not learn from his mistake?" I asked.

Carõ actually laughed, not crazily or angry, just out of a good humor. "Old men don't learn from their mistakes, Zye," he said. "Learn that before you're forced to try and reason with them."

For a moment, I enjoyed the conversation I was having with my brother. It had to be the first in a long time when one of us wasn't angry or not listening; it was pleasant.

In a little less than ten minutes, we reached Raymond's manor, which was made of jet-black stone like the city's wall and took up several acres of land. There were no windows, doors, or even a single light. It was just a mass of black stone surrounded by a huge fence. The fence, unlike the very thick, solid city wall, was thin and short but dangerous. It was composed of closely set eight-foot stakes with razor-sharp points.

"Any ideas?" I asked my brother.

"There must be some way he gets in." He glared at the building. "Come on."

He picked up a stone at his feet and threw it lightly at the stakes. It flew over the stakes and landed safely on the other side; there was no magic on the fence, at least. Carõ was still frowning, though, because we lacked the ability to fly. I did have a sudden idea.

I stepped up to the fence, drew my sword, and slammed it down, hard. At first contact, the blade sliced easily through the stakes as if they were nothing but wood. I was about to question Raymond's intelligence in home security when the stakes suddenly grew back. In less than a few seconds, the four or five stakes I had cut were taller than their originals.

"Here," Carõ said, advancing on the fence with his own sword. He sliced through about six of the stakes and then, without waiting or looking at me, took a running leap over the now-three-foot fence. As if in anger at the man's quickness, the six pegs shot back up to over ten feet.

"You have to be quick," Carõ told me through the fence. "Just cut them and jump unless you want to get impaled."

"Right." I nodded. I glared at the black stakes for a moment and then hacked down five before me. At once, I ran forward, wrapped my hand around a neighboring pole, and propelled myself up and over. I landed steadily on the other side, but when I let go of the pole, I found that my hand was burned to the bone.

"Good thing I didn't touch those," Carõ said as we watched the skin reappear on my fingers and palm. "And good thing I didn't melt our swords."

"How are we going to get back out?" I asked as we walked up to the stone wall of the manor. "The third time I cut at the pegs, it almost caught my foot. Next time we probably won't have more than a second or so to jump and land."

"Maybe we should just focus on getting in right now," my brother offered, and I nodded.

We walked up to the solid wall of the manor so that it was an arm's length away. Carõ reached out and pressed his fingers to the stone, sliding his hand along slowly as if looking for something. I could tell by watching his movements that the stone the wall was composed of was flawlessly smooth, almost like black glass.

"Carõ," I hissed, panicking slightly, "it's single-sight glass."

He turned to glare at me, back to his older self. "What are you talking about?"

"This isn't stone; it's glass, clear on one side and black on the other."

"No, it isn't. That doesn't even exist anymore," my brother said, continuing to run his hand over it. "It's just really smooth stone, like crystal. There's no way he can see us."

I still wasn't convinced, but I allowed him to continue in silence. I was sure it wasn't stone; even crystal had to have imperfections. This was glass. Even if it wasn't single-sight glass, it still couldn't be rock. I shivered at the thought that Raymond Green was watching me at this second, laughing at my brother's attempts to enter his home. I stopped and stared at the black sheet before me. I glared at the perfect house positioned so awkwardly in the poor area of the city. So close to the wall.

Suddenly, Carõ hissed in excitement as the tips of two of his fingers vanished into the wall. A half smile passed over his lips as he succeeded in passing his entire hand through the solid foundation. Without hesitation, he walked right through the wall. After a short, slightly confused moment, I followed him.

"How did you know that was there?" I whispered, but Carō made a shushing sound so soft it could have been a breeze against a windowpane—had there been any.

It was almost completely pitch black inside. The only light came from a dim lamp hanging on a door off toward the left. Carō pressed a finger to his lips and motioned for me to follow. Together, the two of us darted silently toward the door, swords out and ready. With each step my heart pounded a little harder to the point that I was surprised my brother couldn't hear it. Three feet from the office room where the light came from, we stopped. I could hear Raymond talking to himself in a low murmur and the slow, steady, cringing slice of a blade on a sharpening rock. *It was glass,* I thought wildly. *He saw us and is now waiting for us to come in. That sword's for Carō and me. Just like it was for Shintie.*

15
CHAPTER FIFTEEN

I took a breath and allowed the tip of my blade to tap the back of Carõ's leg. Even under the thick armored clothing he wore at all times, I knew my brother felt the metal because he took another step forward. He nodded, despite the fact that he was standing in front of me, and we leapt into the office. Raymond Green looked up at us, grinned, and placed the sharpening rock down on a desk.

For about a half a second, I studied every feature I could take in. He was tall, thin, and thickly muscled. His dark hair was slicked back with thread, and he wore a black armor shirt and leather plants. His eyes were black and scarlet and bloodshot, but just around the rim before the whites I could almost see a misty-gray color. He looked, only for a moment, as crumpled as his city. Then he stood up, readied his sword, and proved just how tall he was.

"Well, well," he said. His voice was amazingly light for having killed so many people. I guess you just get used to it. "General Carõ and the little brother. Tell me, young man, what was your name? I don't remember it."

"Zyemen," I said after a moment.

"Zyemen?" Raymond repeated. "Let me guess, you prefer Zye, do you not?"

I didn't answer.

He turned back to Carõ when I didn't respond. "I've been wanting to speak with you, actually," he said. "I'm glad you're here."

"Unless you're about to tell me you're handing Sandstiss over, I'm not interested in what you have to say," growled my brother.

Raymond chuckled. "You may have my city if your brother can defeat me." He actually offered me an encouraging smile. "Come on, young man, follow in your brother's footsteps."

Losing my temper and not even trying to control it, I raised my sword and ran forward. I wasn't angry enough to have that weird control of time like when I had attacked Carõ, and I didn't yet know how to use it voluntarily, but I was still a talented swordsman. I dove at Raymond, facing the tip of my blade at his chest and almost hitting the mark before I was about toppled over with a counterattack. The king swung his own blade around like a club and pushed mine away as hard as possible. Carõ stepped up to and began to fight, but he wasn't angry and desperate for blood like me; he was just dueling almost as if to humor me. This realization fed the flames in the back of my mind, and I regained my lost ground in a violent leap.

As the fight started to drag on for minutes rather than seconds, Carõ would several times use his left hand to push me back out of the way. My first thought was sarcastic; for not wanting any part in revenge of his brother, he sure was doing a lot of the fighting. However, I quickly learned his reasoning. In training, practicing with Tayer, playing with my brothers, or even in Silver, I had never in my life seen a swordsman like Raymond. He was everywhere at once. His sword flashed around almost too fast for my eyes to follow. Carõ had been right; he was too much even for both of us.

The desire for revenge, however, was greater than my fear of skilled fencing. I dove at the thick blade with mad energy and no plan. I used the flat side of my sword to try and knock away Raymond's, but Raymond was much stronger than I. Every time I made an attack, no matter how powerful, it was nothing against the king.

After almost fifteen minutes of spinning around each other, slamming blades, and trying to kick Raymond's legs out from under him, both Carõ and I were exhausted and drenched in sweat. His arm swung wider each time Raymond beat it away, opening him to even more attacks. I'd never seen my brother take on and not defeat an opponent—until now.

However, it wasn't until Raymond kicked Carõ hard in the chest so that he fell to his back that I started to really become worried. His head was the first to collide with the hard floor, and it made a sickening crack. Raymond stepped over my brother and stomped on his right hand, his sword hand, with a booted foot. I winced when I heard the bones crunch, but Raymond just chuckled at my brother's shouts of pain and held his sword over Carõ's throat.

"Carõ!" I said, the blood freezing in my body. I had once before seen someone hold a sword to my brother's throat with the intention of death in mind, but that had been me. Watching the same act by someone else, someone I hardly knew, was completely different. He had just killed one of my other brothers, and I knew he wouldn't hesitate in doing it again.

"Don't worry, Zye," Raymond said. He bent slightly to tap the end of his blade against Carõ's throat. "I'm not going to kill your brother."

With that, Raymond offered him a free hand and pulled him to his feet. When Carõ was again standing, I saw his face had changed. His eyes were bloodshot and tinged with scarlet, his pupils were contracted to bizarre-looking slits, and his mouth was turned up in an insane (or should I say, more insane than was usual) grin. Raymond had somehow managed to gain control of him. *A thousand-year-old king and a powerful general against a teenager,* I thought madly. If I hadn't been doomed earlier, now I was.

I knew for a fact that I couldn't take on both of them without getting as close to death as possible. The only option I had was to run. It killed me to be a coward, but I had no choice. I backpedaled out of the office, turned, and sprinted for the door. Behind me, I could hear two pairs of boots coming after me, and I ran even harder, pounding my feet against the hard tile. I collided with the black glassy wall. For a few desperate seconds, I tried to find the passageway we'd entered through but failed. There was nothing but solid blackness.

Carõ caught me first. I felt his thick arm close around my neck and throw me to the ground. Choking for air, I scrambled for my sword, which had flown from my hand, but all my fingers found was something hot and wet. Something hit me, harder than I knew was possible, on the side of the head, and I blacked out for a second. Carõ's sword came into my vision. With failing hopes, I tried to push it away with one hand. I watched it slice open my palms and shirt, staining the white cotton red. The loss of blood, more than anything, was making it hard to remember what I was doing, let alone focus or even see.

The thing that hit my head slammed me in the side, breaking ribs. I couldn't scream from pain because I was sure something had happened to my vocal cords. An overwhelming wave of humiliation swept over me. I had watched the best soldier in history die at the hands of Raymond Green, and I had for some reason I couldn't explain anymore thought I stood half a chance against him. I was unsure if I was dying or about to lose consciousness, but there was nothing more I could do. Before I was completely gone, one last thought touched my mind. *I'm sorry, Shintie,* said a voice that didn't sound like mine. *You taught me everything … and I learned nothing.*

Carõ stood there for a moment, watching his brother's lifeless body with a twinge of disgust. He stopped his concentration on his eyes and could almost feel them return to normal. His vision became perfect as it had been before.

"He isn't dead, is he?" came Raymond's voice somewhere to the left.

"No," the general said with reassurance. "No, he's a Draes."

"That explains a lot." Raymond entered his vision somewhat to the side. "I wondered if he was. That's why you want him dead?"

"If there were only a way to kill the Draes and not him," growled Carõ with frustration. "He'll be the first of, what, thousands?"

"At least." The king sheathed his still-bloody sword. "But war means death, death means victory, and victory means peace."

"Among all the cities," the general said, his spirits lifting some. "Now there's just the matter of what to do with him until they can die."

A low chuckle escaped Raymond's lips, and he smiled. It was the kind of half-insane smile that Carõ use to shrink away from. That was, until his began to match. "He can pay my son a visit."

16 CHAPTER SIXTEEN

The only reason I knew I wasn't dead was that I was in so much pain. If I ever got there, death would be painless and peaceful. This wasn't peaceful. My head pounded viciously, and my side and stomach (where I knew a sword had pierced the skin) were hot with blood and searing with agony. I knew the rest of my body was also covered in bruises and wounds, but now that I was once again awake, they would probably start healing. Slowly, I forced back stiff eyelids to find myself surrounded by dim green lighting.

As I stared up at the sky, I tried to take in my surroundings. I was lying on my back on ground that was so soft, it had to be grass. Grass was something Tahll had told me about once. Made up of tiny, bladelike leaves sticking out of the ground, it hadn't grown on X48 since before Raymond's time. That fact alone sent a stab of terror through me, because it probably meant I wasn't on my home planet. Above me, most of the sky was hidden by thick, dark emerald trees of a kind I'd never seen before. They had thick, fat leaves with wide trunks covered in moss. The very tops were probably a hundred feet away at the least. The scene around me was so peaceful that for a moment, I wondered if I had been wrong and I really was dead. But my hopefulness was destroyed when I tried to sit up and about passed out again with a fresh wave of pain through my head. I didn't understand, though, why my head was so painful. It should have begun healing by now.

I made another attempt to move, but this time I ignored the throbbing in every muscle in my body the best I could. Using the entirety of my arm strength, I forced myself into some kind of sitting position. Before my vision could adjust to what I was looking at, the pain in my head and chest intensified. I wrapped an arm around my torso and lost my balance. My elbow hit the hard ground, and I keeled over to my side. My foot hit something hard, and my eyes flew open again.

A few feet away lay a thick black boot. Attached was a young man toying with a hunting spear. He was watching me intently, one eyebrow raised and lips upturned in something of a grin. A thin, ropy scar traced down the right side of his face. "Easy, soldier," he told me. At once I recognized his voice and matched it with his appearance. "Stay down until you have the energy to move without knocking yourself out again. Can you talk at all?"

"I know you," I started stupidly, forcing myself back onto my back instead of lying on my side.

"I know you as well," he said. "You are Zye, am I correct?"

"Yes." I paused. "I don't remember your name, if you told me."

"Ash."

"Where am I?"

"Not X48," he said, "but I never named the planet. I figured if I wasn't the first here I had no right to name it."

I sighed and stared up at the trees. "Why are you helping me?"

"I can leave you, if that's what you want," he offered, "but personally, if I were in your place, I would want a guide who knew the area and the creatures who lived in it."

"Is this place dangerous?"

"Very." The change in his voice forced me to look over at him; somehow, his white face had darkened. "I don't know what animals lived in Hishe, but they're nothing like the things I've found in this jungle. Things you could never imagine until you've seen them. I've lived here for a decade, and I'm not sure I've met every type of creature on the planet."

"Is it all a jungle?"

"For the most part, but the only variation is water." Ash paused to consider something. "I have never in ten years met another human on this planet. How is it you ended up here so injured?"

"I was trying to kill Raymond Green, and he was too strong," I said, watching the sky again.

"What problems did you have with Raymond, Hishen soldier?" The man laughed lightly.

"He killed my brother."

"Oh." The grin vanished. "I'm sorry to hear that. He was a soldier?"

"Yes, the chosen soldier of Hishe."

"That's not good," he noted. "Was he replaced?"

"Yes, by me," I said. Saying it out loud, I was crushed by a new wave of emotion: embarrassment, humility, and guilt. I was supposed to defend Hishe with my life, not run off like an overconfident child. I shut my eyes, not believing how thick I was.

There was a long moment of silence before either of us spoke again. In that time, I realized there was a small fire hanging over us, suspended in the air. I couldn't believe I hadn't seen it earlier. "How is that possible?"

"What?" In the silence, Ash had begun to sharpen a rock with his shoulder knife.

"That fire." If I could have pointed, I probably would have, but I couldn't. "What's holding it up?"

"Nothing." Ash shrugged. "I put it up there to ward off any unwanted guests. It wouldn't scare off a legend creature, but really only jaguars live around here."

"Legend creatures?" I asked, thinking back to Austin. "Like a wolfer?"

Ash laughed, back in a good humor. "Thankfully, no. I've never seen one of those, and 'legend creature' probably isn't the best term to describe them. There are just some things on this planet, like I said before, that can't really be explained. They're not human hybrids, but they're smarter and stronger and faster than animals."

"Have you ever met one?" I asked, enjoying the man's company more and more.

"Face-to-face or just watching it?"

"Face-to-face."

"Once. I don't remember it very well because it was about seven years ago, when I was still charting the planet. I was hunting, and I found these weird black footprints. I followed them; they were catlike, and I wanted food. I caught up to it, and at first I thought it was just a big cat, like a jaguar. But when it heard me and turned to face me, I knew it wasn't a jaguar. It was completely black, like a shadow, even the eyes. It was as if something huge had lost its shadow and I had found it. I muttered something in Latin to myself, probably curing my bad luck, and it seemed to understand. None of them have the ability to speak back to me, but they know Latin, and they agreed to allow me to live in peace here. For the most part, we leave each other alone, but sometimes, I can't help crossing the territory and hiding in a tree and watching them."

"Will they be angry I'm here?" I asked.

He looked thoughtful as he considered this. "I don't know; I hope not, for your sake."

"They'll kill me?"

"They'll do their best if you upset them."

The laughter that escaped my lips was real amusement, something that seemed rare anymore. "They'd have a fun time trying; I die hard."

"Draes aren't immortal, Zye, and there are a lot of things here that are a lot stronger than you," Ash said, looking up from his knife and rock and seeing my shocked expression. He chuckled darkly again. "Yes, I know you're a Draes, don't be so surprised; you're not the first I've met. You are the first I've met who isn't careful about his tag, though."

"What?" I mustered, suffocating under a new wave of confusion.

"I knew you were a Draes from the second I found you facedown in the dirt about four hours ago," he explained. "When Draes die for the first time, when their heart stops beating and starts again, their tag changes. The letters that make up their name transform into a name symbol: one shape. It's not a word or calligraphy; it's a symbol unique to one man, you. Yours is neat. Look at it."

With some of my strength back, I was able to push myself into a sitting position against a tree. My right hand was shaking too hard to use, but my left was undamaged enough to pick up the metal tag around my neck. I forced my head down, once again swimming in pain, and glared hard at the new inscription that had replaced "Zyemen." Carved solidly in the metal was a large Z shape with two lines coming out of the diagonal line to the right. I fitted my thumbnail into the grove of the symbol and traced out each letter.

"Did you know you were a Draes?" Ash asked lightly.

I nodded, not moving my gaze from the shape.

"You should get some sleep then," he advised. "Your wounds will start to heal in that time, and in a few hours you should have the strength to walk. If I'm right, we can spend tomorrow heading back to my home, where you can rest out of danger until you're yourself again."

"Then what?" I asked, letting my head lean back against the tree bark.

"Then either you'll go hunting with me as payment to my kindness to you, or you'll leave and I shall never see you again."

"Both," I assured him, closing my eyes. "But you are an intelligent man, so let me sleep now and see if what you think about a Draes is correct."

"I knew a Draes as a close friend," Ash said. "He taught me about them. Maybe I could do the same for you."

"Maybe," I said. I tried to stay awake longer to learn more about this strange man, but I was much too tired to stay awake. My injuries and strained mind pulled me under, and I was out in seconds. Over the night, I kept seeing Carõ, face twisted in mad anger and doing his best to kill me. When morning came, even though I knew it had been more than twelve hours, I still felt exhausted and weighed down as if I hadn't even closed my eyes.

Suddenly, my thoughts were interrupted by the low undertone of a voice. I recognized it as Ash's at once, but I couldn't decide if he was talking to me or himself. I hadn't really given any sign of life yet, but then again, he had realized I was still alive when I was facedown in the dirt, dead. I tried for a moment to listen to his constant, rhythmic speech, but I couldn't understand it. It was both too low to hear clearly and too fluently Latin.

Giving up on eavesdropping on Ash's conversation with himself, I announced my consciousness. "Good morning."

"It is," Ash said, completely unfazed by my interruption. "Do you have any more strength back?"

"I think so." I flattened my hands to the soft grass and pushed my feet under me. Leaning against the tree I had slept on for support, I forced my legs to straighten and hold up my weight. With a great deal of effort and holding on to a branch for dear life, I managed to find my feet on my own.

Ash laughed and clapped his hands together. "I'd say you do have your energy back about you!" He paused to throw me a slightly burned strip of meat. "You must be hungry by now."

It turned out that I was not just hungry but completely starving. It wasn't until now that I realized that I hadn't eaten anything since my trip home from Silver. I couldn't even remember how long ago that had been. I felt like some kind of animal tearing into the meat as if I'd never seen it before, but Ash only watched silently and tossed me more when I finished.

When I was finally full, he grinned good-naturedly, "Now you're definitely going hunting with me," he told me. "I'm pretty sure you just ate a whole something."

"Thank you for it," I said, pushing myself away from the tree and nearly toppling over. "I don't know if I can hunt yet, though."

"I wouldn't doubt that," he said, handing me his spear to use as a crutch. "We'll spend today making it back to my home, where you can rest a little more out of danger. Tomorrow, we'll go hunting; two days should be enough for you to get the entirety of your strength back."

"I can't thank you enough for your help," I said, trying to sound genuine.

"You don't need to thank me with words like a child," Ash said, not trying to hide the irritation in his voice. "You're a soldier. Thank me tomorrow and prove you learned something in that ruddy canyon of yours."

For some reason, I couldn't help taking slight offence to his comment; the way he spoke about Hishe angered me. I was beginning to think he might be more than an ambassador.

Ash shouldered a long bow, handed me my sword, and drew on his black cloak. As we began walking, I realized every move he made was totally and completely silent. His boots had to be metal plated, and still they landed on the leafy grass as lightly as air. His cloak never flew up with the breeze and caught on branches or vines. He ducked easily around anything that might lay in his path, leaving it as perfect as it was for me. I, on the other hand, crashed clumsily and noisily through the underbrush and probably scared off any prey within a ten-mile radius. Ash, however, said nothing. I knew I was probably driving him insane with my level of stealth (or lack thereof), but he didn't show it. After about a half an hour, he began talking, and he managed to speak almost nonstop for the remainder of the several-hour-long walk.

I have never in my life met a man who could talk so much to an almost complete stranger. For about an hour, he explained about his time here, how he had learned to hunt like a wild creature and avoid the planet's dangers. How he had discovered his magic abilities were so much stronger here than on X because he was the only human. How he had developed methods of riding the faster creatures and stalking calmer ones. It seemed that he knew almost everything that could be possibly known about the planet.

"You're patient to listen to me for this long," he said after speaking for about five minutes on one breath. "You'll understand that you're the only human contact I've had in ten years."

"So does that mean you are not an ambassador?" I asked.

"No," he said after a moment. "I ran away from Sandstiss when I was very young. I feel compelled to apologize for the lie earlier this year."

"It's fine," I grunted, wishing I could walk better with his spear. "I'm honestly interested in this place, but do you have any idea how much farther we're walking?"

"Are you tired?" Ash grinned.

"Well," I said. I paused to lean on my "crutch" for a moment and wipe the sweat from my face. "I'm not really awake, if that's your question."

"Actually, we're here," he said, chuckling. "Look up."

I did. We were standing at the base of an immense cliff face shooting up at almost a ninety-degree angle. It reminded me of Silver, but there were no rocks jutting out to climb up, and it wasn't nearly as tall or steep. I was about to ask Ash how he planned to get up, but he twisted his hand around at his side and forced it back with a quick motion. The reaction was a stony ledge jumping out from the cliff face, just wide enough for two people. I took in a fast breath when I realized that was the exact same thing I had done on Silver and that it had taken a good deal of exertion even for a Draes. All the magic Ash did was completely effortless.

"I figure you're not in shape to climb by hand?" He grinned, stepping onto the platform and waiting for me to do the same.

"You'd figure right," I told him, watching the ground get farther and farther away as he circled his wrist around, pulling us up.

In a matter of seconds, we were above the tree line, and I could see just how extensive Ash's planet was. Dark green trees, wide rivers, and gray mountains seemed to cover the entirety of the landscape. After minutes of climbing, I still couldn't see the bend of the horizon. I wondered for a moment if the planet wasn't round.

After almost five minutes, the dark shadow covering us from the mountain died. We were at its peak. I turned around to see a wide hollow blasted away in the stone. It almost looked as if he had set off an explosion in it. Could magic really do that? Inside were a number of weapons in the process of being made, crude clothes, white wooden planks, meat, and a few other handmade articles.

"Home sweet home," he said, retrieving a strip of cloth and throwing it to me. "Here, that head wound's going to kill you if you don't let it heal. It's not as bloody as yesterday, but it still looks pretty bad."

I let out a breath of air through my nose and tied the cloth under my hair around the lump on my head. I wiped the dry blood from my face and the back of my neck, noticing that my hair had grown almost to my shoulders. *How long was I out?* I wondered, fingering the strands. *I could tie this back if I wanted.*

"Would you give me an answer if I asked you a question?" I asked, putting as many words as possible into the first one.

Ash pressed his lips together in thought until he said, "It's dependent on what the question is, but most of the time I'm pretty open-minded."

"Are you going to kill me because I'm a Draes?"

The reaction to my question was not what I had wanted or expected. Ash as good as fell to the stone floor and rolled out the cave mouth, he was laughing so hard. "Why would you ever consider that? For what reason would I waste my time, my food, and my supplies in bringing you back to the living just to kill you again? Why would I kill you for something you, your father, or your father's father couldn't control?"

"I don't know. Most people seem to want to kill Draes," I said defensively, trying to ignore his insane mirth.

"Do I seem like most normal people to you, Zye?" Ash asked me.

I chuckled; this man honestly didn't care that I was a Draes. "You said you knew another Draes before." I paused, wondering if I was being rude. "Who was it?"

"Why do you ask?" He yawned and kicked off his boots into a corner.

"I don't know where my father is," I said finally. "He either died or vanished when I was very young, so I wondered if he could be the one you knew."

"The Draes I knew was an old man who lived in a highly guarded prison in Sandstiss; I doubt it was your father."

"There's always hoping." I chuckled. "By the way, there's something I couldn't help noticing about you."

He waited.

"You're voice is almost like Raymond's. It's really faint, but I can almost hear his accent when you talk."

"Really?"

"Yes." I nodded. "Did you know him?"

There was a long moment of silence, and I wondered if I had gone too far. This man had, after all, as good as saved my life. I wondered again if I was being rude. I watched him for a while, trying to read the emotion in his face, but there didn't seem to be any. Was he mustering some kind of courage?

Finally, he said, "I'm Raymond's son."

17
CHAPTER SEVENTEEN

For a moment, I stood stock-still, not knowing what to think. If I was angry, it wasn't directly at him. It was at his father, and for Ash's being who he was. I wanted to kill him because I'd failed at killing his father. If I was confused, it was only because I knew Kyre. He was also a prince, but he was a spoiled, rotten, rich man's son who received everything he wanted. I knew that if Ash was who he said he was, he didn't have the life Kyre took for granted. He wasn't the typical prince I'd heard so many stories about; he didn't have shining armor and handsome robes. He didn't have a belt sword and sheath made of gold and black metal. From what I knew about him, he hated Raymond and was ashamed to be his son.

"I'm going to return your question, Zye," he said, still not looking at me. "Are you going to kill me?"

I pressed my lips together, thinking for a minute. "No," I said. "You're right; you can't change who you are. I think I'm starting to realize that."

"Good." He turned to face me, his expression light again. "Get some sleep. It's going to rain tomorrow, and we're going hunting; you owe me a catch."

"I'll warn you now, Ash," I told him, thinking of Henner. "I'm a downright awful hunter; I can't keep quiet to save my life in the woods."

Ash gave a combination of a laugh and a yawn and leaned easily against the stone wall. "It's a good thing we're not going to be in the woods, then," he noted. "I'll bet this is the first time you've ever been in a jungle. Besides, it's a lot easier to be quiet here; I'm not much use in a forest either."

"I wouldn't think there was a lot of difference," I said, half asking for clarification.

Ash shrugged and changed the subject. "Have you ever used a spear before? Or a bow and arrow?"

"I learned to fight with both, but the one time I went hunting I had a sword."

"It's not too different," he said, "just aim and throw." He then picked up his spear. He twirled it once in his hand and then launched it with physical strength alone into the gray rock. It wobbled a little at impact until he yanked back out and threw it back with the weapons. I noticed then that none of his weapons was a sword.

"It's pretty easy," he said. "I'll show you in the morning."

He was about to fall asleep when he straightened up as if remembering something. It was a little too dark to see well, but it looked as if he were poking himself in the eye.

"What are you doing?" I asked, laughing a little.

A light appeared in the cave at that moment, illuminating the two of us. Ash was holding his hand near his face, balancing something clear and small on his forefinger. "I'm blind in my right eye," he explained. "This is like the glasses the Earth people wear, but it actually sits on my eye."

"Does it give you sight?"

"Not really," he said, placing the little sheet of glass in a pocket on his shoulder. "But it makes things blurry, which is better than gray."

"Is it because of your scar?"

"Yeah, the sword that cut up my face cut through my eyelid, pupil, and iris." He continued, "You can kinda see it, actually."

"Kinda" was an understatement. When I watched his eyes for the first time, I realized that the red line of his scar did cross through his eye. The iris had a black line running down it that had scattered some of the gray color into the empty pupil. The majority of his eye was a dim, foggy color—the color blind eyes were. He blinked, showing an awkward slice through the skin of his eyelid. The two fragments had tried and failed to heal back together, leaving one down farther than the other. The white of his eye was a pale pinkish-red color, almost as if it had been dyed.

"That looks painful," I told him, backing up a few steps to retreat to the wall again.

Ash laughed coldly at this, and the light in the cave faded out. "It was ten years ago," he said. "When it first happened I was just in shock, but the next day I was in more pain than you were yesterday. I was pretty sure I was going to die, and fear and pain are not a good combination."

I knew that was true. Fear and pain didn't help any situation separately, much less together. I was still tired, though, and I didn't respond. I slid down the wall and leaned my head back against the cool rock. Several yards off, Ash straightened up a little, crossed his arms lazily over his chest, and shut his eyes. After a few minutes, he was snoring, still standing. *This man is so strange*, I thought, unable to think of a single person who could keep his balance while sleeping. I could hardly sit up and do it. I unbelted my sheath and set it down as quietly as possible. It had been getting dark ever since we'd entered the cave, and now it was almost pitch black. I couldn't see any stars out, and the green sea below was just a mass of black. Slowly, I closed my eyes and reopened them to enhance my vision.

The instant I could see, I doubled over in pain and slammed my eyelids shut. It felt as if someone had clubbed me in the head with a metal rod. I kept one hand clenched on the edge of the cliff for balance and the other on my forehead, nails splitting the skin. In the back of my mind, some kind of hazy image formed. It was Raymond, a crocked grin on his face. Then his features transformed … to his son's.

I forced my eyes open again. The pain vanished as quickly as it had come. For several minutes, I knelt on the cold stone, panting breathlessly and using the remainder of my energy to keep my eyes open. My face was hot and sweaty, and my arms shook violently from their cramped position.

"What was that?" I whispered to myself. "No wound has ever hurt that much!"

"You all right?" came Ash's voice suddenly, slightly concerned.

Behind me, it was too dark to see details of the young man, but his outline looked like Raymond. I shook my head and pushed myself shakily to my feet. This man was Raymond's son; how could I even justify trusting him?

"I know you don't trust me," he said, as if reading my thoughts, "but Zye, I'm not my father, and I'm not going to turn you over to him. He gave me this scar on my face. He was going to kill me, and he hates me as much as you hate him for killing your brother."

I stood in silence for a moment, trying to ward off the attack about my brother.

"Get some sleep," he said, returning to his place of rest, "and don't use magic. You probably got that headache from using magic before you're back to one piece."

I feel as if I'm being warned, I thought, sitting against the wall. *I've never had a vision like that; that wasn't a dream. How could it have been a dream? I wasn't asleep. Do Draes have visions?*

I slept with my sword close at hand that night. Every time I startled and woke up, I would panic for a second and scramble for my hilt. Several times I dreamt that Raymond was looking for me and Carõ was at his side. I knew my brother wasn't evil; Raymond had managed to control him somehow. That wicked look in his eyes wasn't his; he'd been doing what Raymond wanted because he had no choice. The thought that this was his fault did not and would not cross my mind. When the sun finally rose, I was tired and restless without having had much real sleep. I felt stronger, though. The pain in my head had pretty much ceased to exist, and the small wounds were nothing but fading red marks. The bloody knot on the back of my head was smaller but still painful. Overall, I was back into one piece and strong enough to hunt.

I stretched my stiff arms and pushed myself to my feet. Over to my left, Ash was still snoring loudly, slumped upright against the wall. I belted my sword on and stood in the mouth of the cave. Off in the distance, I could see dark storm clouds forming. A flash of white fork lightning struck a tree but only produced smoke. The air smelt like rain, but the scent was not similar to that on X48. I wondered curiously why Ash needed the rain to hunt and how he knew it was coming. *Wouldn't animals go underground in the rain?* I thought.

The cool air felt good on my face, and I closed my eyes, enjoying the single moment of calm. I knew that as soon as I got back to X48 I had to find Carõ and then Raymond, but I was stronger than before; I could feel it.

Suddenly, I heard, "Got ya!"

A strong foot kicked me in the back of the legs, sending me out into the open air. I twisted around just in time to grab the cave ledge. Looking up, I saw Ash, laughing his full head off and offering a hand.

"Remind me of your age again?" I asked, accepting his help up. He took all my weight easily in one hand.

"Twenty." He paused. "I think. I'm not completely sure. It takes about a year for that sun to turn around; there's a dead spot on it, so each time I see it, I say I'm a year older. Obviously, I've caught it ten times. By the way, you don't need that sword."

"You don't hunt with a sword?" I knew the answer, but I didn't understand it. "It kills soldiers. Why can't it hunt game?"

"Can you throw a sword a thousand feet?" he asked, handing me a spear. "This is the same thing as a sword, but you can throw it farther."

I gripped it in the middle, held back my arm, and launched it at the wall. It made hard contact, and the head drove into the stone. The wooden part cracked and splintered violently. I glanced at Ash, who was incredulous.

"You broke my spear!" he said, making an attempt to pull it out but only managing to completely detach the wood from the white, pointed head.

"Sorry about that, Ash." I glanced around for another hunting weapon.

He wrenched the head out of the stone, laughing. "It's fine. I guess your strength is back. Oh, one more thing."

I raised an eyebrow, taking another spear from him.

"I told you my name was Ash only because it's the name I gave myself. My father called me Aspen, but I don't want you to call me that," he said. His face was dark again. "I left that name with X48 and Raymond, when I left my old life ten years ago. Call me Ash."

"I like that name more than Aspen anyway." I grinned. "Ash has a meaning; Aspen is a word." I paused to study the strange white boards I had seen last night. "What are these?"

"Surfing stars," he said without looking around. "They're like riding stars, only permanent; they don't vanish."

"It's so long and heavy." I lifted one with my foot; it had to weigh eighty pounds at least. "How on X48 does it fly?"

"It actually flies about five times faster than a riding star." He grinned. "It's my own invention."

"You invented that?"

He nodded. "Like my glass eye sheet."

"Would you mind?"

"Not at all." He knelt to pick up the star with no effort and handed it to me. "Just throw it out. It'll come back fast, so jump on it."

Easier said than done? You bet. The star was almost impossible to lift, let alone throw, and it seemed to like Ash better than me. Each time I got it in the air, it would shoot forward and circle back to him. It took a good ten minutes to even get on the thing, but Ash was patient. When I was finally on, gripping the edges with both hands for support, he grinned and nodded.

"There you go," he said. "Now just ride it like you would a riding star. One warning, though: they're really fast, and they don't accelerate."

I was about to ask how something didn't accelerate, but my question was lost when I leaned forward the slightest bit and was launched forward, moving probably thousands of miles a minute. The sharpest turn I could make to go back to the mountain was the size of a small barn, and seconds later, I was less than a mile away from the cave and coming in too fast. I made a desperate attempt to stop or at least slow down, but in less than a quarter of a second I was going to crash right into the back of the cave. Luckily, I felt something grab the back of my shirt and rip me off the star. In the middle of falling to the ground, I saw the surfing star collide with the back wall. When Ash had control of the star and I was sure I wasn't dead, I looked up to see him roaring with laughter again.

"You okay?" he asked, offering a hand to pull me to my feet.

"Yeah," I muttered, watching a fresh gash on my arm heal itself. "Did you do that only because you knew I'd crash?"

"Not entirely." He grinned.

"I bet you wouldn't be laughing so hard if you had the task of bashing my head in," I said, grinning slightly. The intense speed had made me slightly dizzy.

"You think a teenager with one year of training is a match against a man with ten years of fighting experience?" Ash was still laughing in a good-natured way.

I frowned, taking some offence to the accusation but deciding to continue the conversation as it was. "I've been training since I was five; I can handle any weapon."

"Save for a spear?"

I really wanted to slap the smirk off his face. "Wars aren't fought with hunting spears."

"They were against the dragons."

"That was hundreds of years ago, before anyone knew how to hold a sword or create a powerful curse with magic. Anyway, how do you know about the dragon wars?"

"I did have a few years of formal education," he said, snickering. "I retained about enough to make coherent sentences and sound smart … sort of. I just didn't get a rich man's son's education."

"Don't say anything against my father," I warned, trying to deflect the blow. "Let's go."

I didn't look at Ash; I just waited for him to speak again.

"Challenge accepted," he said finally, grabbing a spear from a stockpile. "Tell me when you're good enough to fly and fight at the same time."

"How fast was that thing going?"

"About five hundred thousand miles a minute," he said plainly. "Even a Draes would probably get some kind of concussion, and you're no good to me unconscious."

"All right," I said easily, fitting the spear in a strap over one shoulder on my back, another of Ash's inventions. "Let's go."

Ash grinned. "Eager, are you, mate?"

The last time I'd been hunting, I hadn't done very well; yes, I was eager to try again.

We rode the ledge-elevator down to the forest floor and moved quickly and soundlessly over the soft grass. Well, Ash was soundless. Even with my energy back, I was still clumsy and off balance in the jungle. As we walked, though, Ash was totally speechless for the first time since I had met him. Everything about him was quiet. I saw a wild, dangerous look in his eyes. It wasn't like when Carõ was being controlled by Raymond, with black and scarlet eyes, fierce with excitement. Ash looked crazy, but his eyes were still their natural gray color. Natural gray—Raymond's eyes were gray. It was the first time that I had noticed they were the exact same shade. Even under the blinding mist in his right, the iris was the same dark, stony shade as his father's.

"Why are you watching me like that?" Ash asked suddenly, turning his head to fix his gaze on me.

"I'm not," I said quickly. "I was just thinking your scar must be painful."

He glared at me in confusion. "I've told you, it is. You don't need to gawk at it." He paused. "And walk on my right, will you? Remember, I can't see anything over there."

For some reason, I had thought the man would want me within sight. I hadn't even considered he would use me as extra vision. It calmed down my distrust of him a little that he trusted me that much. I nodded to him, fixing my head straight forward, and passed behind him to his other side.

"Thanks," he said. "I'm not accustomed to having a hunting partner, but I …" his voice faded away, leaving the statement unfinished.

I was about to ask what he was suddenly so intently watching, but he turned to me and grinned. "You ever rope a horse?"

I raised an eyebrow. "Yes, why?"

He didn't answer, just took two loops of rope from over one shoulder, handed one to me, and shook his so that it transformed into a lariat.

"Should I be concerned?" I asked, shaking my own rope but accomplishing nothing. "How did you do that?"

Again, he didn't answer, but he pressed a finger to his lips and moved aside. I hadn't even noticed, but we had come across a large clearing, and in it stood two enormous beasts.

They were seven feet tall, each with a thick black coat and massive lionlike manes. Two long saber teeth protruded from either side of their mouths, making the three-inch fangs behind them look harmless. Small ears that lay flat to their skulls were accompanied by short, almost hidden, horns that were positioned backward and horizontally to the ground. On their long, sleek paws were razor-like claws easily capable of slicing a sword in half. Their dark, thin bodies were long and streamlined, as if they were built for high speeds and sharp turns.

They were lounging in the tall grass, grumbling back and forth as if talking. So far, it didn't seem as if they had noticed us.

"This is a bit like roping a horse," whispered Ash, "but it's a thousand times harder. Also, these guys are going to try and kill you; they're not flight animals like what you're used to."

This didn't surprise me; they had no reason to be flight animals. Even without the horns and saber teeth, they were still seven-foot-tall jet-black lions. The only reason I say "lions" is because I honestly have no other word. They were built like huge wildcats in the tail, paws, and face, but they were like no cat I'd ever seen in my life—or heard of. Was this one of the creatures Ash had been talking about?

"I thought you said the creatures you found didn't live around here," I said in an undertone.

"They don't. These are just hybrids," he explained. "The creatures I was talking about have some supernatural abilities, like control over the elements."

"So are we hunting these?"

"No," he said with another evil grin. "They're our rides."

Keeping to the shadow of the trees, Ash stepped silently out from the safety of the dense undergrowth. Slowly, he readied the loops of his rope and raised it to eye level. Thirty feet from the first, taller creature, he jerked back his arms and threw the rope without warning. The thing looked up just in time to watch the makeshift lariat fall around its neck. It roared angrily and charged at Ash, sabers and claws flashing. The second creature shot its head up at the commotion and scanned the area. At first, it only saw its fellow, struggling with the black-haired man, but then it saw me.

With a violent growl, it lunged fiercely toward me. There were about fifty feet in between the lion-saber-tooth-tiger and me, giving me about three seconds to react. My brilliant, soldierlike, quick-thinking reaction was to slam my single rope loop against a tree and curse angrily at it when it didn't duplicate into a lasso.

When the thing was on me, much more effective soldier instincts kicked in. I grabbed two handfuls and the thick front mane and threw myself around the massive head. It turned back as quickly as I had, already facing me before I even found my feet again. Somehow, I needed to get on it bareback and get the rope over its head. I tried taking more fur as a handhold, using the actual coat and not the mane this time. The creature roared, not in anger but in pain, and twisted around on its hind legs. The violent motion threw me off and into a tree. I landed on my stomach, my back searing in a quick pain, and was momentarily rained on by a series of twigs and leaves.

I shook the debris off, grabbed my rope, and pushed myself to my feet. The black mass of fur and teeth was bolting across the field toward me, having shot me clear to the other side like a dead weight. I found Ash with a quick scan of the area; he had the lariat back into a loop of rope around his own ride's neck but was backpedaling violently in order to avoid getting smacked in the chest by a heavy paw a foot in diameter.

"Have you done this before?" I half shouted. We were pretty much back-to-back now in the middle of the field. The two creatures were closing in on either side.

"A thousand times, probably more." He laughed. "Don't worry: riding's harder!"

"What are they, anyway?"

"I call them black sabes."

"Got a plan?"

He nodded. "When they're a foot off, jump left and grab the rope. I'll get his attention, so he'll swing at me. The force should launch you up."

They were now fifteen feet away. "What about you?"

"It's a surprise."

They were now five feet away, then three, and then one. I dove off and latched both hands on to the tan rope. Just as Ash had predicted, the sabe jumped to the right, swinging me on bareback. I adjusted my seat quickly and held the rope reins with a death grip. Ash, still on the ground, dodged the huge cat with impossible ease and turned back to his cat. He threw out one hand at it, ran forward, and jumped. His outstretched hand landed on the thing's muzzle, and it froze. Every muscle down to the whiskers stopped instantly. Ash glided upside down over the sabe's head and twisted around to land forward. When his hand left the coarse fur, the charm vanished, and it bolted forward.

For a moment, all I could do was stare at him in amazement. "I know healers who can't pull that off," I said in shock. "You're one hell of a magician."

He gave a sideways grin and tugged on the makeshift reins. "The fewer people you've got on a planet, the more powerful you become. I said that earlier. You know, I did feel my strength go down about a week before I found you. That's actually why I was hunting on foot; I figured I might meet somebody, and I didn't want to steamroll them by hunting on one of these guys."

I laughed and followed him. The black sabes were hard to control but ran at top speed. They reminded me of training a fresh stallion, but they were much faster than any horse I'd ever ridden, even Starra. In the dense undergrowth, they would dodge and lean and jump obstacles without any warning, almost unseating me every time. They weren't quite as stealthy as Ash was on foot, but they didn't need to be. I found that leaning low against the sabe's back allowed me to hold on better as well as avoid taking low-hanging branches to the face. When I figured this out on my own, Ash laughed and pointed out that, for once, I didn't look like a proper English schoolboy on a rich man's horse.

There was a difference between the sabes and horses, even compared to Starra, which made me enjoy riding them more. I felt as if I had halfway melted into the thick fur, and I was no longer telling the huge beast where to go but was actually making the turns and jumps myself. Top horses like Starra and war horses could reach speeds of over seventy miles per hour on an open field. In the thick rainforest, the two sabes were probably moving close to something like eighty or ninety, easily able to overtake anything they come across. This was why, after almost three hours of riding, I was starting to get concerned. The black sabes hadn't noticed anything to hunt—or if they had, they'd given us no indication. They continued straight on for three entire hours, mine following Ash's.

"Ash!" I shouted finally when I'd had enough of the silence. "Where is everything?"

"I dunno," came his muffled voice twenty feet ahead of me. "They haven't pointed at anything."

I waited for a moment as we bolted through; even if we weren't quiet enough to avoid giving a heads-up, we were still too fast for something to escape.

"Want to go on foot?" he asked. "That way we're using our own eyes."

"Yeah, let's go."

I released my hold on the rope and slid backward off the hind end of the animal. It seemed to realize it was free, for it took off even faster, probably hitting over the hundred mark in speed. I landed on my feet and staggered forward to catch my balance. Within seconds, both sabes were gone.

A second later, Ash came back at a petrified dead sprint. Behind him, the air was rent apart with a flash of white lightning and a deafening explosion of thunder that rattled my eardrums.

"Go!" he shrieked. "I was wrong about the storm!"

A single raindrop hit my sweaty face, but it wasn't cool. It was boiling hot, and it felt as if it were burning my cheek. A second hit my shoulder, and it burned and sizzled violently on the shredded cloth. I saw a water bead hit Ash square on the top of the head, and he clasped a hand to it painfully. A moment later, the rain become steadier and heavier, and every glass crystal that touched the leaves of trees or blades of grass exploded into a tiny flame that grew and devoured everything. Ash ran past me, grabbing a handful of my shirt, and pulled me forward into a run. There was no way we were going to outrun a storm of fire.

"Ash, are you crazy?" I yelled over the pounding rain. Somehow, we were about ten feet in front of thick clouds and managing to keep the lead for almost five minutes. "We rode for three hours; we can't run back to the cave!"

"We don't need to," he panted. "Just run—and follow me."

I had run fast before, mainly in training and with Tayer, but never had I moved this fast on foot. The instant the front of my boot met solid ground, I locked my knee and propelled myself forward. The branches hanging low in our path continually slapped me in the face and chest, almost as if the surrounding woods didn't want us to outrun the storm.

"Come on!" His voice was almost deafened by the pounding gale behind and around us.

We were on an actual path now; it wasn't much of one, but it was still a path to follow. We followed it for about twenty seconds. The rain was just overtaking us when Ash suddenly disappeared. He had dived headfirst into a vast lake that extended outward for miles. The water was glass clear with millions and millions of tiny explosions of raindrops all over its surface. The boiling hot drops burst into puffs of gray and black smoke when they hit the cool lake water. I watched Ash's dark figure dart through the pool, took a breath, and followed him.

18

CHAPTER EIGHTEEN

The water under the surface was cool and not extremely painful on the fresh burns. With my eyes open, I could see for miles. The lake was alive with plants and fish ranging from tiny guppies that could fit in your hand to huge sharklike creatures probably fifty feet in length. Above, I could hear the muted sound of the storm pounding the water's surface as if the burning rain wanted to reach us. I didn't know how long Ash could hold his breath, but I knew I couldn't outlast a wide storm.

Once again, though, Ash proved his perfect knowledge of the planet. We dove deeper and deeper until my ears were burning from the pressure. After a few minutes, we came across an opening in a cave about a foot wide. Ash squeezed through, and I followed blindly.

Inside, it was empty. The stone walls were bone dry, and the room was full of oxygen. It was a little bubble of air safe from the weather and water. For a moment, we just sat there, sopping wet and panting, too breathless to form words.

"Nice," I said after I found air in my lungs again. "Is there any part of this planet you don't already have mapped out?"

"There's a very small area where I'm forbidden from going."

"Forbidden?" I stared at him questioningly. "I thought you were alone?"

"I am, for the most part." He wrung out his black hair casually. "But like I said, those creatures on the other side of the planet aren't too friendly."

"I thought you said the storm was prime hunting weather," I said, beginning to wonder if having lived totally alone for an entire decade had had some effect on Ash's sanity.

"Normally, it is." Ash's face was dark, and his voice suddenly serious. "I wasn't expecting that to happen. Zye, I rigged the storm clouds on this planet seven years ago to rain fire when someone landed here. It didn't go off for you because you were dead and you didn't land, you just appeared, but someone else is here. This isn't good."

"Maybe it was an accident?" I asked hopefully. The distressed look on Ash's face was starting to worry me. "Maybe someone landed here to rest while traveling?"

"I don't think so." He pulled his leather jacket off to dry it with magic and did the same to his boots and cloth shirt. "Nobody's found this place in ten years, and suddenly I get two visitors? I don't know much about you, but I do know that the man you were running from never stops on a hunt."

"Are you saying you think I led your father to you?"

"I'm saying there's someone here. I don't know who, and I don't know why, but there is someone on this planet who shouldn't be here."

"How long until we can leave, do you think?" I asked, trying to lighten the mood slightly.

"Whenever the water stops tiding in the hole we came through," he said, pointing out how the water lapped up a few inches, retreated, and returned over and over. "In still water, it wouldn't be doing that."

"Is that because of magic you did?" I asked, watching it for a moment.

"Yeah." He paused. "About a month after I rigged the storm clouds, I realized I didn't want to get caught in it unexpectedly. I found this underwater ridge and blasted a hold in it. Somehow, it keeps oxygen on its own, though. That's helpful."

"It can hold enough for the two of us for the whole time?"

"Definitely."

"So what now?"

"We probably have a few hours." He leaned back on his arms, more relaxed. "Why not get to know each other a little more?"

I paused, apprehensive. "You first."

A small smile crossed his lips. "As you already know, my father is Raymond Green. I've never met my mother, and I am his only son. For ten years, I was raised by a young woman who lived as one of the servants in the manor, and she became one of my only friends. When I was three, I received a colt I named Everlife for a long life expectancy and taught myself enough Latin to speak with him. You know, of course, that some powerful magicians who know enough Latin can sometimes communicate with animals? Anyway, I mastered riding, arrows, the sword, hand fighting, shoulder knife, and so on by age nine, so I wasn't totally defenseless. My father knew I was a strong kid, so on the night he planned to kill me, he came with ten guards to accompany him. The woman who had raised me warned me, and with a five-minute start I left the city on Everlife.

"It wasn't more than an hour's ride before the eleven men caught up to me. I was completely surrounded. Eleven fully grown men, armed with swords and years of fighting experience, surrounded a nine-year-old boy to kill him. Can you even think about that? I knew I could fight, and I knew I could ride, but I knew I couldn't defend myself and my horse and escape with my life. I dismounted and yelled at the stallion to run. He was out of sight in seconds, so I knew he was safe. He was smart enough not to return to Sandstiss. With Everlife gone, I pulled out my sword and faced my father, who also had his blade drawn. He and the guards dismounted, and they all pulled weapons.

"'You are a brave man, Raymond Green.' I laughed to him, preparing myself. 'Even if you were alone, how is a child a match for a trained man?'

"'Life is hell, son,' he said to me, and he walked up to me ready to kill his only kid.

"For a few seconds, I held my own. For half a minute, I fought a man almost a thousand years older than me and didn't fail. But then, he wasn't taking it easy on me anymore—well, easier. He destroyed my sword and sliced my face in two. At that point, I knew I couldn't win. The vision in my right eye was totally gone then because of all the blood, and my shoulder had been jammed out of its socket; I was going to die if I stayed. I hated to be a coward, but I conjured a riding star and left. I left my father and his guards, I left my city that now had no future leader, and I left X48. Forever.

"I couldn't travel very far, only far enough away from X48 so that my father couldn't follow me, and I landed on another planet much like the one I'd left. I was so disoriented that I thought I'd just circled X and landed on it again, and I tried to fly off again. I got about fifteen feet in the air before I passed out and the star I'd made rammed me in the leg. When I woke up, I was in a dark, cramped room, and my first thought was that I was dead. But then, you know, you realize how much pain you feel, and you know you're not dead. Death, whenever it comes, is apparently painless.

"At that moment, a little boy with brown hair and an innocent, kind expression pulled back a door and filled my little closet with light. He explained to me that his name was Keith and he was the prince of Golden City, the only city on the planet we were on. The planet had always kept to itself, and when he had found me, he was terrified I wasn't alone. He'd been riding outside of the city's walls and seen something huddled on the ground; that something was a nine-year-old boy with a dislocated shoulder, a broken kneecap, a cracked rib, and a bloodied face. He brought me back to his father's castle (it's like a huge manor house) and hid me in his clothes closet.

"After a few weeks, my bones healed, and my face was relatively human again. In that time, Keith and I became good friends and learned a lot about each other. I learned that his father had died when he was younger (he was six when I met him), and until he was thirteen—the age for a prince to become a king if needed—his uncle would be king of Golden City. He was a good, honest man and wasn't too angry at his nephew for finding me. He had a young women help Keith in restoring my health, and I lived in the city for about a year. I didn't want to leave, but I knew I needed to; if the citizens of the city learned about me, they might not like it. Keith and his uncle gave me a new shoulder knife and some gold in case I should find a new planet with a city to live in. I told them I doubted it, though; I was finished with society, and I'd always liked being on my own anyway. So I left Golden City and, for three weeks, traveled on a riding star out through the middle of nowhere. I passed only a few stars and even fewer planets, most of which were uninhabited but not fit for life. It wasn't until the end of my third week that I found this planet. I saw the lush green and rivers and landed at once. I rested near this lake for about a day and then started exploring.

"There's not really much else to tell; I found my mountain, blasted out an opening to live in, and mapped out the rest of the planet. Ten years later, I thought I'd try and go back, to see how Sandstiss was doing, but I just couldn't do it. I was so close, as you know, but I couldn't force myself to face Raymond after all those years. So I'm alone. You're the first human I've seen in all that time."

He finished his speech not looking at me. He was staring misty-eyed into the little window of water, watching the tiny waves lap over the dry stone. I looked at his face and noticed again just how damaged it was. We sat in silence for a moment until Ash tapped his finger on his knife and let a drop of blood hit the crystalline water.

"The Draes I knew told me something once," he said, watching it disperse. "Once you're strong enough, you won't even lose blood. Wouldn't that be nice."

I didn't know how to respond to the sudden change in topic, so I simply noted to Ash how strange a man he was. This earned me another loud laugh.

"You're one of the only ones I know, so I can't make a judgment," he said, pressing his thumb to his bleeding finger to stop it. "And it's your turn … what's your story, rich boy?"

What was my story? I was pretty normal, or at least I had been. "I'm the youngest of five brothers, and two were soldiers. Now one's dead and the other's a famous general. I'm a soldier, and I've finished training and school and everything. I've mastered dozens of weapons and riding styles, and apparently I fight like my father. My father left me when I was three, and I've never seen him since. After your father killed my brother, I went after him, and somehow I ended up here. After that, I guess you know the rest."

"You aren't very interesting," he mused. "The life of a Draes is supposed to be full of adventure and excitement."

"My apologizes." I chuckled. "I didn't realize there were rules."

"Oh, but there are." He was serious again. "You can't get angry, you can't get close to someone, you can't hurt someone you love, you can't let your existence be known, and you can't, more than anything, use a Stone Sword. They're all infused with dragon venom or blood, and even letting the blade touch your skin could mean death."

"My brother, the historian, he told me Stone Swords didn't exist," I said. Even the name "Stone Sword" made me cringe. "They're real?"

"Oh, yes," he said. "And there are only four in existence, two of which are safe under the Hishe manor."

"Under?" I asked.

"They're in a clay coffin under the foundation," he said.

I wasn't sure what disturbed me more: the fact that the prince of my city's enemy knew exactly where the most powerful weapon in existence was or the fact that it really existed in the first place. There was also the idea of the swords being buried with someone dead, because that was the only way to close up a clay coffin for good.

"What about the other two?" I asked, unsure if I wanted the answer.

"Under the manors of Loca and Marlo," he said. "Sandstiss hasn't held one since they were created. They were originally meant to be the weapons of each chosen soldier, but I'm sure that dream died a long time ago."

"If they're so deadly, could I use one?" I asked.

Ash shrugged. "Depends on how strong you are. The old man I knew back home tried once, and he about burned off his hand."

I made a mental note not to try.

At that moment exactly, the water was still. It wasn't even something we had to notice; we'd both been watching it eagerly when it suddenly stopped moving. The drop of blood that had spread thin in the window of water now hung motionless as if frozen.

"If this is my father," he said, turning to me with a dark face, "you'd better hope he doesn't have a Stone Sword."

"Is there a way he would?" I asked, slightly more terrified than before.

Ash shrugged halfheartedly. "I think that by now, he's proved he can do just about anything."

"If Raymond plans to kill me and has the ability," I said, wishing I had my own sword on me now, "at least I'm taking him with me!"

"I just hope you can." Ash prepared to dive back through the water. "For your sake. Oh, one more thing."

I waited.

"That rain turned to fire, not just boiling water; it creates kind of a big, projective bubble over my mountain."

"Or a blaring, outright 'this is where I am; come kill me' sign," I said without humor in my voice.

Ash glanced up, grinning. "You really have a problem with paranoia, don't you?"

"That's not being paranoid, Ash," I said, "If there's someone here to hunt us, you basically just told him where we are."

"It's also the only warning I have," he said, slightly irritated. "Remember, I live alone. Now, you can hide here and blame me, or you can follow me and face whatever or whoever found this planet."

"I'm coming," I said. "Let's go."

Ash dived headfirst through the little glassy window of water, and I followed his feet. We pushed our way through the lake with Ash angled so that we were also moving toward the dark mass of the shore. As the surface came closer and closer, I noticed a lot of red and orange and not a lot of green. Still fifteen feet under, my vision blurry and unfocused, I realized what Ash had been trying to get at. The rain had turned to fire, and now the whole forest was a huge inferno.

I broke the surface and took a second to regain my breath. Once my lungs had oxygen again, I stared forward and was paralyzed. Trees were alive in flames, the bushes and plants were being eaten alive, and birds shot from trees to a safer area of the planet. Next to me, Ash looked disgusted. His lip twitched violently, and there was a half-mad, half-helpless look in his eyes.

"That's my home," he said, shaking his head. "No one's ever come here, so I only imagined what this would look like. This isn't what I meant; I only wanted to scare off the intruder. Zye, look what I've done."

"Let's hope it's worth it," I said as we started back to the shore.

Back on dry land, there was no path unblocked by flames. We had to continually shoot water and humid air at the foliage to walk back. We traveled in silence—well, sort of. Neither of us was talking, but there was plenty of sound. The fire crackling and popping angrily, the trees weakened by age and flame crashing down tumultuously, and the air and water rushing from our hands were enough sound alone. We had ridden out from the mountain in about three hours, but the walk back lasted through the night and until late afternoon. By that time, a lot of the fire had turned to smoke, and a normal rain shower was following us. When we reached the mountain base and Ash started the piece of land up its slope, I turned to see his outcome. I could see rain clouds settling in, killing the red-and-orange eating machine on the spot.

"It doesn't look so bad, Ash," I told him as we neared the summit. "What was killed will grow back."

"That's not the problem." He wasn't looking at his planet's destruction. "I don't care if it grows back; I could have destroyed the whole forest. I thought … living here for ten years made me more of myself and not just another human obsessed with killing and gaining for himself … I guess I was wrong."

"You aren't wrong," I said, still watching the blaze. "You were only trying to keep yourself safe."

He didn't answer.

"Ash?" I turned to face him and saw that his face was white. Then I saw why.

19
CHAPTER NINETEEN

Raymond Green was standing with a sword out and ready in the mouth of Ash's cave. He was grinning horribly, and his black cloak, so much like his son's, was burned slightly on the ends. When both of us were facing him, he curled his lips into a devilish snarl. Despite the fact that he was holding a sword, and a rather thin one at that, he had a massive sheath on his back with a black hilt protruding from it. My heart dropped to my stomach as a wave of dread washed over me. I had no real reason to believe it was a Stone Sword, as it should be impossible for Raymond to get one, but I didn't see such an impressive sword as that one very often. My main concern was why he had two.

"You kept me waiting, boys," Raymond said. His gaze was more focused on his son than me, and I had to wonder what it was like for the king to see his ten-year-old as a grown man. Then I remembered that each of them despised the other, and my curiosity vanished.

"I want a rematch," I told him. "You haven't yet died for killing my brother."

Raymond laughed loudly. "Did you not learn your lesson the first time, boy?" he asked. "You cannot stop me; not even the great war hero could!"

"Carõ?" My mouth went dry. "Where is he? What did you do to him?"

The mad king continued to chuckle good-naturedly. "I've done nothing to him, Zyemen. Everything he has done and will do in the near future is of his own accord. Remember that."

I couldn't stand it any longer. I ducked down to grab a nearby spear, drew back my arm, and flung it with both physical strength and magic at Raymond. It landed in his left shoulder, about six inches off target. The force of the blow wasn't enough to cause Raymond to fall, but it did buy me the time I needed to dive for my sword. By the time I was back on my feet, blade in hand, Raymond had pulled the weapon free from his arm and was making his way back toward me. It more than unnerved me to see that not only was his arm completely healed already but there was not a drop of blood anywhere.

"Ash," I called, closing the remaining distance between the king and myself. Ash was a few feet to my right. He didn't have any blade but ended up being quite talented with his shoulder knife. The three of us spun on the spot for several minutes, hacking and slashing at each other with desperate violence. I was unable to wound Raymond badly, and most of what I received healed in the seconds after it was delivered. Occasionally I would hear Ash shout in pain or surprise, but he held his own fine, so I didn't feel the need to worry.

After some time, Ash and I had somehow managed to back Raymond against the ledge of the cave. There were several distant clangs as his sword, which he had dropped, fell to the jungle below.

Panting slightly, I raised my blade to his neck and stared at him without blinking. "Is there anything you want to say, Raymond Green?"

"If only it could be that simple," Raymond said. He was shaking his head, *laughing*.

The complete lack of fear in his eyes fed the flames of anger in my mind. "Go to hell," I snarled through my teeth.

"I would if I could, Zye, but I'm already there thanks to your brother. If only you'd allow me to end this now."

"End what? You? Believe me, I'm about to!" I snapped.

"You still don't understand." There was a soft, pleading look in his slightly gray eyes. "It's Carō, not me."

"Liar!" I shouted; I'd had enough. I didn't care about Raymond's accusations of my brother, be they real or not.

In the same instant that I was about to kill Raymond, he reached up and wrenched the thick sword from its sheath. There was one single break, an instant where our swords met, clashing against each other with a violent explosion of sparks. I swung around the too-heavy blade frantically and, without a second thought, drove it forward directly to Raymond Green's heart. With satisfaction, I saw blood and knew I had wounded him fatally. Letting go of the hilt, I lifted a leg and kicked him in the stomach, pushing him from the edge of the mountain.

I leaned over and watched him fall, a faint smile upturning my lips. "It was always you."

20 CHAPTER TWENTY

I didn't for a second allow myself to believe that it could possibly be that easy. When I turned to face Ash, he seemed to be thinking the same thing. He replaced his knife in its sheath and covered the remaining feet between him and the cliff.

"Come on!" he said roughly, jumping from the cave mouth. I didn't pause this time to think. I had decided to trust Ash a while ago, and I was willing to bet that if he was jumping to his death with me, he wasn't planning on dying. With a running start, I pushed myself from the stone and turned in the air to face downward. About fifty feet below me, I could see Ash, his dark cloak billowing around him. Any attempt I made to call his name was lost in the rushing air.

When he was about in line with the tops of the tallest trees, I watched him hold out his arms and slow down enough to land without breaking bones. I heard him shout, probably by magnifying his voice, for me to do the same. With some difficulty, I forced my arms up and stopped instantaneously midair. I quickly discovered that lowering my arms allowed me to fall again, and I fell and slowed for three-quarters of the remaining height. When I was only about twenty-five feet from solid ground, Ash made a movement with his hand. I heard him say something in Latin, and I dropped the remaining distance.

We had landed in a small clearing, fresh ash floating around us like snow. In the very middle of the field lay the crumpled figure of a man. He was motionless on his back with his eyes closed as if sleeping. Apart from the hole in his chest, there wasn't a scratch on him, not even from falling.

"Is he dead?" Ash asked curiously, nudging his father's boot with his own.

"I'm not sure." I shrugged. I noticed my blade lying beside Raymond and picked it up, careful not to touch him with it. It still had blood on it, which meant the king was injured if not dead, and he didn't look as if he would get up anytime soon.

I saw Raymond's sword sticking out of the ground a few yards away. As Ash crouched down to watch the dead man for any sign of life, I crossed over to it. Closer up, I realized it wasn't only his blade. Wrapped around the hilt was a dog tag, or at least what I thought was a dog tag. It wasn't silver and pentagonal like everyone else's; it was jet black and triangular. The bottom point was sharp enough to be a deadly knife. I lifted the edge on one figure and actually cut my skin on the point. The rim of the tag was as razor sharp as the ends. *If this is Raymond's,* I thought, *how on X48 did he wear it without cutting himself open all the time?*

The answer, however, was obvious when I focused on the carving in the metal. It wasn't his name, an occupation, or even a letter; it was a strange symbol I had never seen before in my life. I knew I didn't recognize it, but it had a sense of familiarity that assured me what it was and answered every question.

"What's that?"

I jumped when Ash spoke suddenly beside me and closed my fist around Raymond's tag. Luckily, he didn't notice the black shard in my hand, being too focused on the sword.

"It's Raymond's." I shrugged. "I guess he dropped it."

"What should we do with it?" he asked, eyeing it as if it were some poisonous animal.

"Maybe for now you should carry it," I said, pulling it out of the soft soil. "I use my father's blade, and I hate him."

I offered the sword, the hilt pointing at him, and for a long moment he didn't move or speak. Finally he said, "I don't trust this sword; it's killed too many people. People who weren't even soldiers or enemies."

I had to stop myself from laughing. "It's a sword, Ash, and you need one. All weapons are meant to kill. What your father did with this blade doesn't affect what you will. The same has gone for me for fourteen years."

Ash sighed heavily and took it from my light grasp, examining its every detail. He took a strong vine from a nearby tree and looped it over one shoulder as a makeshift sheath.

"We should go home," I said when he was finished, "to spread the news."

"And what about me?" Ash looked concerned. "Do you think Rainwin is just going to let me live with you in Hishe?"

"Actually, I was thinking you would return to Sandstiss," I said. "Would you not agree that those people—your people—deserve a better king?"

Ash shook his head. "They deserve better than Raymond or me, but for now I suppose you're right."

"You already sound like a better king than him," I said. "Let's go."

As Ash returned to his cave for two surfing stars and some other supplies, I opened my hand to stare down at the little black tag. Despite the razor-like edges, my hand was amazingly unharmed. It wasn't even bloody. I didn't know if Raymond Green was what I thought he was or not, but I was more than sure that without this strange tag he wasn't coming back for revenge anytime soon. Just to be sure, however, I snapped my fingers, and the remaining grass the fallen king lay upon lit up in flame. It reached him in a second. I turned away from Raymond Green and my memories of my oldest brother. I grinned to myself as the forest lit up again and I climbed back up to Ash's cave on foot.

To be continued …

ABOUT THE AUTHOR

Rachel Carter, currently a rides operator at an amusement park, is a senior at Lakota East High School. She marches a sousaphone in her school's marching band and shows a Western quarter horse named Whodunit Dee Lux. This is her first published book, and she is hopeful for its success.